A Candlelight Ecstasy Romance®

"I'M NOT GOING ANYWHERE UNTIL WE'VE TALKED THIS OUT," RAPHAEL INSISTED FIRMLY.

"What's there to talk about? Nothing's changed. You're still the same man I left in France. You have to be the center of attention, don't you? First, when you were on the soccer team, and now as a sex symbol to millions of women. A Ferrari, a penthouse—you've even got the same types of expensive toys you had back then. But that's not enough. Oh, no, now it's driving in the Dallas Grand Prix. When will you grow up?"

"I *am* grown up, Gabrielle. Remember the last time we were together."

Driven by fear, she lashed out at him. "Being a good lover doesn't mean you're a man."

Raphael recoiled, almost as if she had hit him. Then his chin became set. "Gabrielle, someday you'll understand. You may not believe this, but driving in the Grand Prix is the most adult thing I've ever done. And I'm doing it for us, for our future."

CANDLELIGHT ECSTASY ROMANCES®

SCARLET MEMORIES

Betty Henrichs

A CANDLELIGHT ECSTASY ROMANCE®

Published by
Dell Publishing Co., Inc.
1 Dag Hammarskjold Plaza
New York, New York 10017

Dell ® TM 681510, Dell Publishing Co., Inc.

Candlelight Ecstasy Romance®, 1,203,540, is a registered
trademark of Dell Publishing Co., Inc., New York, New York.

ISBN: 0-440-17618-2

Printed in the United States of America

First printing—July 1985

To Mildred Dashen, a mother whose love, caring, and understanding over the years is a gift I deeply cherish.

To Our Readers:

We have been delighted with your enthusiastic response to Candlelight Ecstasy Romances®, and we thank you for the interest you have shown in this exciting series.

In the upcoming months we will continue to present the distinctive sensuous love stories you have come to expect only from Ecstasy. We look forward to bringing you many more books from your favorite authors and also the very finest work from new authors of contemporary romantic fiction.

As always, we are striving to present the unique, absorbing love stories that you enjoy most—books that are more than ordinary romance. Your suggestions and comments are always welcome. Please write to us at the address below.

Sincerely,

The Editors
Candlelight Romances
1 Dag Hammarskjold Plaza
New York, New York 10017

CHAPTER ONE

"Raphael, don't!" Gaby O'Shea giggled as the icy rivulet of champagne trickled down between her breasts.

"What's wrong? I thought you liked champagne," he murmured, bending to sip the sparkling liquid from her skin.

When he'd chased the last drop, he tipped the bottle again, sending a cool stream into the hollow of her neck. The darting probe of his tongue, dancing, tasting her flesh, sent a delightful shiver through her, warming her blood far more than the champagne had cooled it.

"This is insane!" she protested weakly as his lips moved over her throat.

When the last drop had disappeared, Raphael lifted his head. "Why Gabrielle? You know I love Dom Pérignon."

The way his Spanish accent rolled over the words brought a smile to her lips as he continued, "It's even better after it's been sweetened by touching you. Yes"—he chuckled softly, tilting the bottle again—"it's making me thirstier by the second."

"Want me to get you a glass?" she teased. "That way you can drink it faster."

"True, but it wouldn't be half as much fun as sipping it from your delightful body."

This time Gaby gasped as the cold stream flowed down over her stomach, stopping only when it reached her bikini bottom. The touch of his lips, the stroking of his tongue as he traced the edge of the fabric, turned her gasp into a moan. The sound echoed her defeat, a defeat she knew would be sweet. With a happy sigh she laced her fingers through his black hair, letting the familiar blaze of desire burn away any further protest.

It felt so good, so right, when Raphael touched her, when he loved her. Every nerve within her sprang alive, letting her live, enjoy, experience, completely. No other man had ever possessed the magic to arouse this urgent need within her. When Raphael touched her it felt as though he'd captured the heat of the Mediterranean sun for her pleasure alone. As his hands caressed her that heat flowed through his fingertips into her, heating her flesh until every part of her was scorching with a desire only his velvety thrusts could cool.

His strong fingers slipped beneath the band of her bikini, lifting it away from her skin. "Hmmm, looks like several drops of champagne strayed down here. You're always telling me not to waste money, and Dom Pérignon is definitely too expensive to waste, so I guess I'll just have to follow the trail."

As he starting tugging her bikini bottom down over her hips Gaby's hands stopped him. "Raphael, wait. Let's go inside. What if someone sees us?"

He propped himself up on one elbow so he could gaze down at her. "Who's going to see us?" He waved his hand at the grounds surrounding the villa he'd rented. "This patio is very private, and I gave the servants the night off. There's no one to see us but the setting sun. And speaking of that sun, my prudish Gabrielle, when are you going to become

10

fashionable?" he teased, flicking the top of her emerald green bikini with his fingertip. "We're in Saint-Tropez. Why don't you take your top off like all the other women? Worship the sun with your *entire* body."

"Sorry, I'm from Texas. There we do our sun worshiping in private. Besides, where's that notorious Spanish jealousy of yours. I wouldn't think you'd enjoy having other men gawk at me."

"Maybe I just want them to envy what I have and they can never possess." He laughed the laugh of every conquering male. Then his smile faded. "And I want a taste of that sweet possession right now," he murmured as his fingers searched for the hook to unfasten her bikini top.

The sun, glinting off her diamond wristwatch, winked at her, reminding her of their plans. "Wait, Raphael, we can't. There isn't time. Niko is expecting us on his yacht at eight, and I have to bathe, do my hair, and—"

"Do your hair? Why?" he asked, his eyes darkening to the blackest obsidian as he looked at her. "I don't like it when you wear it up. I love the way it falls free and soft, like a velvet cloak across my shoulders, after we make love." He lifted a strand of her long hair and wrapped it around his finger, studying it. "It's such an unusual color, like the costliest port wine. No other woman in the world has hair this color. It intoxicates me. Then I look into your eyes and I'm really lost."

He ran a fingertip beneath her eyes. "They call this part of France the Côte d'Azur, the Azure Coast, and you've captured all its beauty. Eyes as mysterious, as compelling, as the sea—no wonder Jean-Claude lured you off that runway in Dallas and made you his star model. Tonight Saint-Tropez, as well as Paris, will fall at your feet."

"It won't fall if we miss Niko's party. The invitation said it starts at eight, and—"

The amused shake of Raphael's head silenced her. "Ah, you compulsive Americans. Always slaves to the clock. What is time? Nothing but a manmade straitjacket. In Spain we let our desires rule. If we want to eat, we eat. If we want to sleep, we sleep." He paused, his voice deepening as he reached with a finger to touch the pulse throbbing wildly in her throat. "If we want to make love, we love. Nothing else is more important. Shall I prove how it works, my Gabrielle?"

Raphael was right. The party on Niko's yacht would go on all night. Why ruin the delightfully scandalous feelings that were making her body tingle now? Gaby stretched, mimicking the moves of a cat. As she moved she deliberately rubbed her body invitingly against Raphael's.

"I don't know," she said, running her toes with provocative strokes up his muscular leg. "We Americans are as stubborn as we are compulsive. I may be hard to convince."

"I've got hours and hours to try," he vowed, gathering her tightly into his arms. "And, my prudish Gabrielle, the moon of Saint-Tropez is no more inclined to gossip than the sun, so be free," he urged, burying his face in the warmth of her neck.

"Be free? Okay, if that's your wish, my handsome *caballero* . . ." she teased, reaching across him to pick the bottle of champagne off the table.

Before he realized what she intended to do, she poured the sparkling wine over his chest. He blinked, surprised, then a satisfied smile touched his lips. "Ah, so I've convinced you of the way to heighten the—"

"Raphael, be quiet," she urged, bending to lick the sweetness from his body.

Bronzed by the sun, his body hardened by endless hours of exercise on the soccer field, his muscles rippled over his chest like the waves of the ocean. Intent to learn the mystery of each one, her lips, her fingertips, explored in lingering strokes as her kiss moved down, then up, then across his body.

Finally, when her sharp nip found the hard nipple buried in the lush black hair curling across his chest, he shuddered. "Gabrielle, what you do to me with your kiss, a stroke of your hand . . ." The words came out between pants of breath. "Each time is new, like the first. Come here, kiss me; the champagne is almost gone. Besides, what I have for you is sweeter than any wine."

Gaby refused to be tempted. "But, my friend, weren't you the one who advised me to ignore time? Why hurry?" she asked, reaching for the bottle of champagne again.

The tight black swimming trunks stretching tautly over Raphael's hips riveted her attention as Gaby drew away from him slightly. Her eyes, seduced by his obvious desire, lingered long moments, savoring what would be, then moved downward. The tickling of champagne bubbled over the heavy muscles of his legs. She smiled, running her hands over his thighs. "Raphael, can I make a confession?"

"What confession, Gabrielle? Don't tell me you have thought of some other interesting ways to use the champagne!" He chuckled. "Tell me. So far I love what you're doing!"

Gaby moved so she could look at him. "No, it's not that. It's about your legs."

"My legs?" he asked, obviously confused. "What about them?" He paused, staring at her. "Gabrielle, I don't believe it: You're blushing."

"What is it they say—you can take the girl out of the country, but you can't take the country out of the girl. I guess that's me. I still blush when I'm embarrassed."

"What are you embarrassed about? My legs?"

"No, just how they affect me," she admitted hesitantly. "Jean-Claude is a soccer fan. I'd never seen a match, so he took me. I saw you in that world-cup match in Paris. Spain against France. Remember?"

"Sure, we won three to zero, but—"

"And you scored two of the three goals for Spain," she interrupted. "But it wasn't just the excitement of seeing that. Raphael, I couldn't take my eyes off of you. Out there, running around the field in those tight shorts, your legs, all muscles, passing the ball, ramming the ball in for a score . . ." Gaby hesitated, swallowed, then continued. "I couldn't stop thinking how it would feel to have those legs wrapped around me, making love to me, pouring all that strength into me."

She lowered her eyes, embarrassed by the intensity of what she'd experienced. "I'd never had thoughts like that before in my life." A shudder of pleasure rippled up her back as she glanced back at him. "It was wondrously frightening."

"So now I know the truth: You're just another soccer groupie." He laughed. "No wonder you had Jean-Claude introduce you to me at Countess Frederika's party."

"Raphael, no, I'm not like all those other screaming women that follow you everywhere you—"

He stilled her protest with a soft kiss. "Gabrielle, shhh, I was only teasing. You're like no other woman in the world—certainly not like those women who throw their hotel-room key at me when I leave the field after a match." .

"Have you ever been tempted to catch one?" she joked, her smile easily returning.

"No, you're the only one that tempts me. And you're tempting me a whole lot right now."

"I know." Gaby smiled, reading the desire sparking his gaze. "I can see it in your eyes." She tilted her head to one side. "You said I have eyes reflecting the ocean; well, yours are much more primitive. Eyes of a hawk—that's what they remind me of. Powerful, jumbling my heartbeat with only a glance. They're ever-changing, sometimes cool, like the darkest hours of the night, hiding many secrets. Sometimes, like now, they're hot, like blazing coals. It may have been your legs I noticed first, but it's your eyes I'll never forget."

Raphael kissed her gently, deeply moved by what she'd said. Then he drew a breath. "I'm glad I affected you as strongly as you reached out to me. I'll never forget the way you looked when I first saw you." Raphael nestled her closer against him as he admitted, "Since we're making confessions, I have one of my own to make: Even if you hadn't shown up at Frederika's party, I would have found you."

She shook her head, confused. "Why? How? I don't understand."

"It's very simple, my beautiful Gabrielle. I wanted to meet you that night just as much as you wanted to meet me. Earlier that day I'd attended Jean-Claude's showing at the Tuileries Gardens with a friend of mine and I'd seen you." He closed his eyes. "The cool maiden, hair of fire, eyes of ice,

15

walking out onto the runway as if you owned the world. A dozen of the top models in France modeled that day, but you were the only one I saw. And do you know what I saw?" He paused as his hand cupped her breast. "I saw the banked passion waiting for the right man to ignite it, and I wanted to be that person. I think we were destined to meet, destined to be together."

"Destined for this night and this moment," she whispered.

"Yes: destined to love," he whispered, slipping his hand beneath her bikini bottom to find the suggestive moisture lurking there.

A soft sigh of pleasure escaped at his touch as Gaby wound her arms around his powerful neck, urging his lips down to consume hers.

The surf pounding against the cliffs outside the villa echoed the beat of the passion rising within her as Raphael's kiss first parted her lips, then plunged deeper. His lips, the thrust of his tongue, the gentle tasting of her sweetness, sent flickers of desire crackling through her, warming her blood like the blazing sun. He shifted his body, pressing her deeper into the cushions of the chaise longue, and she welcomed his weight, wanting to touch, to feel, to experience him totally.

His hands trembled with need when he reached to unfasten her bikini top. As the soft curve of her breast spilled into his palm he drew back so he could look at her. No blush of embarrassment colored her cheeks as he gazed at her lying almost naked beneath him.

"You were right . . ."

The harsh rasp of desire deepening his voice brought a smile to Gaby's lips as he cleared his throat to begin again. "You were right, seeing you

16

like this *does* ignite my Spanish jealousy, as you call it. Even if this is Saint-Tropez, I don't think I like the idea of other men staring at your beauty. Let them only dream about what I can see, caress . . . possess."

To seal his ownership, he bent to place a kiss in the warm valley between her breasts. As his lips moved over her, her skin first warmed, then burned where he touched her. Reveling in the feeling, she arched against him, offering more.

The sensations flowed outward from his caress, rippling through her at first like a breeze-ruffled wave. Then, as his touch moved lower, becoming more intimate, finding the mysteries of her flesh as he tossed her bikini bottom aside, the ripples became swells, and the swells grew in power until she felt as if she were lost in a sea suddenly whipped by a storm. Like someone drowning she clung to him, finding reality only in his kiss, the caress of his fingers, the play of hard muscles against the softness of hers.

Her legs wrapped around him, begging release from the fire devouring her, but instead he held her away. "Ah, my Gabrielle, remember, be patient. Passion is too sweet to rush."

Rolling over on his back, he pulled her on top of him. As his hands cupped her buttocks, lifting her to him, Gaby rose above him. "Now *you* be patient," she whispered, repeating his chant of desire.

To pay him back for the delightful torment he'd stirred within her, she began to tease him. Using her long hair like caresses of velvet, she let it flow lightly over his chest, then brushed it over his shoulders. As he sucked in his breath she moved lower, trailing it suggestively across the sensitive skin of his stomach until he couldn't stand it anymore.

With a muttered oath he threaded his strong fingers through her hair, stopping her. "Gabrielle, you drive me mad! Come, kiss me, love me."

Driven by desire too long denied, they came together in an explosive tempest more powerful than any storm roaring in off the Mediterranean. Every part of her ignited, first smoldering, then blazing as he plunged deeply into her, finally easing the ache only he could satisfy. With her arms clasped tightly around him she let the rhythm of their passion grow, building toward that ultimate pleasure only Raphael could give her. A thousand incandescent candles seemed to sparkle within her as each thrust of his powerful body pulled her higher and higher, until finally, like a wave cresting, they shuddered as one.

The moon, silvery and full, winked down at them when Gaby finally stirred in Raphael's embrace.

"Where do you think you're going?" he murmured sleepily as he tightened his arms about her, drawing her back against him.

"Nowhere," she sighed contentedly. "I'm very happy right where I am, even if we are going to be late for Niko's party."

"How about trying for a *spectacularly* late entrance or, better yet, skipping it entirely?" he suggested, beginning to nibble on her ear.

"Raphael, you're insatiable!" she giggled, as his tongue darted into the sensitive interior.

"Only with you, my Gabrielle. You arouse a desire in me I can't seem to satisfy no matter how many times I try."

The words, blown softly into her ear, began stirring delicious tingles as she protested, "Raphael we can't. I promised Jean-Claude I wouldn't miss this

18

party. He's trying to get Niko to invest in his new signature line, and he wants me there wearing one of his new gowns. You wouldn't want to get me fired, would you?"

"He can't afford to fire you: You're the top model in Paris," Raphael argued, stroking his hand down to cover her breast.

"There's always *after* the party. Didn't you just convince me that patience makes the passion only sweeter."

"Tripped up my own line," he chuckled, stopping his delightful caresses.

"A line? Is that all it was?" she demanded in mock anger. "Hmmm, sounds like the usual Don Juan complex to me. I guess that explains why I always see you in the magazines, surrounded by a bevy of beautiful women."

He grinned, enjoying her teasing. "Can I help it that women find soccer players irresistible? It must be the short pants we wear."

Gaby shook her head. "Personally, I don't think it has anything to do with your being a world-class soccer player. I think it's your name that drives women wild. Raphael Salvaje—Raphael the Savage!" she chanted, translating his last name into English. "What woman could resist that challenge?" A soft smile touched her lips as she confessed, "I know I can't, and there must be dozens like me."

"To keep the record straight, I'm not interested in dozens of women; I'm interested in only one, and I'm going to prove the depth of that interest over and over and over . . . tonight."

"Can all this convincing wait until after the party?"

"It appears I don't have any other choice,"

Raphael muttered. "I guess if you promised Jean-Claude you'd show up, we'd better go."

Reluctantly he rolled away, then stood up. As he held out his hand to help her rise he commented, "At least we won't be bored. Niko always throws a great party, and the *Athena*, his yacht, has to be seen to believed. He has a Van Gogh hanging over the bar, the dance floor is inlaid with lapis lazuli, and there's a helicopter waiting on the top deck in case anyone decides they want to go gambling in Monte Carlo."

An hour later, when she walked outside, Raphael was leaning against the door of his new bright red Alfa Romeo. He straightened up and let out a low whistle when he saw her. "No wonder Jean-Claude wants you at the party when he hits Niko up for that investment. You're so beautiful, you could convince Scrooge to pry open his wallet. I know if I had any loose cash, I'd sure chip it in."

Gaby didn't smile at his compliment. His flippant comment about money bothered her. Raphael lived fast and spent faster.

"If you weren't so extravagant, maybe—"

"Gabrielle, no lectures," he interrupted, opening the car door for her. "This night is too special to spoil with an argument. I enjoy living the way I do, and you didn't seem to object when I rented a villa instead of booking us into a hotel."

She started to say something, then bit her lip. What was the use? Raphael would never change. With a shrug she agreed, "Okay, no lectures. Besides, how can I complain about anyone who buys me Dom Pérignon?"

As Raphael sped down the narrow winding road toward the harbor, Gaby glanced out of the corner of her eye at him. *Maybe the way he lives with such a reckless abandon is part of his appeal,* she admitted silently. *He claims I'm too conservative, too cautious. I guess we're a good balance. Still, I wish he wouldn't spend—*

"Raphael, watch out!" she yelped, automatically slamming her foot down hard as his wild careen around a curve barely missed an oncoming truck.

"No, *you* watch out, my Gabrielle," he countered, refusing to slow down. "I don't want you to put a hole through the floorboard of my new car." He tossed a grin at her. "Besides, why are you worried? You know I'm a good driver. Didn't I race this year in the Grand Prix at Monte Carlo?"

"I know you did. I'll never forget that awful race!" Gaby squeezed her eyes tightly closed as the memory assaulted her. "I still have nightmares, remembering how close I came to losing you that day."

He shrugged, unconcerned. "I saw Pepe's car go into that spin, so I swerved and avoided it. I was never in danger."

"Yes, but what about Pepe?" Her hands clenched, driving her nails into the palm. "I watched him die in that crash, Raphael. Can't you understand how I feel?"

"Look, Gabrielle, you asked me not to race again and I agreed. Doesn't that show you I understand, that I care about your feelings? You know I did it only to get some publicity for the team. It worked. Remember the headlines: 'Spanish Soccer Star Races Death. . . .' "

" 'Races death,' " Gaby repeated. "Yes, that's what you did. And you won, but Pepe didn't. I'm sorry I slammed my foot against the floorboard, but can you blame me for being nervous when you skid

21

through a curve? I've never felt safe riding in a car since I saw Pepe's car explode into flames."

He caught her shudder out of the corner of his eye. "Let's stop arguing about it, okay? I said I won't race again, so just relax. Tell me about Jean-Claude's new signature line. Is he going to take you to New York to launch the line in America?"

Gaby knew Raphael was deliberately redirecting the conversation away from his driving and the crash, but she didn't argue. The last thing she wanted to do was relive the horror of remembering what had happened.

She forced a laugh. "I didn't want to tell you until all the plans were set, but that's exactly what he plans to do. How did you know?"

Raphael reached across the car and curled his hand possessively over her shoulder. "Jean-Claude's no fool. It makes sense that if you're launching a new line, you'd want the most beautiful woman in the world on the runway in your gowns. With you there, success should be a snap."

" 'The most beautiful woman in the world'?" Gaby chuckled. "Be serious."

His teeth flashed white against his dark tan as he smiled at her. "I'm allowed my opinion, aren't I? Anyway, we can argue about it later. Close your eyes."

Gaby blinked at his sudden command. "Close my eyes? Why?"

"Because I want to surprise you. Go ahead, close them."

Remembering the icy stream of champagne he'd poured over her, she laughed as her eyelids fluttered closed. "Haven't you surprised me enough for one day? What are you going to do this time, squirt me with whipped cream?"

"No, but thanks for the suggestion!" He chuckled wickedly as he pulled the car off to the side of the road and stopped.

"Okay, you can open them now."

"Raphael, it's unbelievable!" she gasped when she saw Niko's white yacht in the harbor below. Outlined by hundreds of lights, the *Athena* glistened like some costly jewel against the dark water. Coming from the ship she could hear the sound of a band, and as he'd promised, there was a helicopter waiting on the top deck.

Gaby shook her head as she gazed at the huge yacht glittering in the moonlight. "And I thought Texans knew how to throw their money around. That thing is a floating palace!"

"All it takes to get one is a fleet of tankers. Know where I can pick up a few?"

"You could marry his daughter, Phaedra. I hear her dowry could pay off the national debt. Even the way you spend money, that should keep you in champagne for a while," she teased.

"One more word about my reckless ways and I swear I'll start buying California wine. Then see how you like that!" Raphael laughed as he started the car again.

The steep winding road finally ended at the harbor. As Raphael helped her into the motor launch that was waiting to ferry them out to the yacht, he whispered, "Let's not stay too long. Seeing the way this dress clings to you when you move, makes me thirsty for champagne again."

CHAPTER TWO

Gaby swallowed as they neared the towering yacht. After being in Paris for three years, insecurities didn't often hit her, but this was one of those rare times.

"Brother, this sure is a long way from the Mesquite Rodeo," she muttered under her breath as the motor launch bounced over the waves, taking them toward Niko's spectacular party.

"What is a Mesquite Rodeo?" Raphael asked.

"Well, let's just say you have nothing like it in Europe." She smiled at the memory of the horses she'd left on her parents' farm. "My speciality was barrel-racing."

"Racing barrels?" Raphael inquired with a skeptically raised eyebrow. "You Americans are very strange!"

Before she could explain, the driver cut the motor, letting them drift toward the side of the ship.

"Watching you climb up that ladder should be *very* interesting!" Raphael joked when the boatman turned away to secure a line.

As she started up the ladder Raphael's hands slid up her silken-clad legs, not stopping until they reached the sensitive area along the inside of her thigh. "Raphael, don't! You're going to make me fall," she protested with a giggle. "Jean-Claude would be furious if I took a tumble into the sea. It would ruin his gown."

" 'Raphael, don't!' " he mimicked, starting up the ladder after her. "That seems to be your favorite phrase lately. Why spoil the fun?"

She glanced back over her shoulder at him and winked. "Can't you wait?"

His black eyes flashed with a sudden blaze of wanting. "Not when I'm waiting for you! *Insatiable* is not a strong enough word for what I feel when I look at you. And touching you is even worse!"

The beat of passion warming his words, the desire she saw in his gaze, set her pulse throbbing. She smiled at him, letting him know those feelings ran as hotly through her. "Who says we have to stay at the party for hours and hours? With nothing but moonlight waiting for us back at the villa, I can think of another place I'd rather be. Can't you?"

"If I had my way, we'd leave right now!"

"I know the feeling, but—"

Her answer was interrupted by Jean-Claude's greeting called down from the deck above. "Ah, my Gabrielle, so you finally arrive. Now the party shall be perfect. Hurry, there is champagne, Russian caviar, a thousand delights waiting for you."

She smiled fondly up at him as she teased, "A thousand delights, and I thought all you wanted me here for was to impress Niko so he'll back your new line."

"You wound me, Gabrielle," Jean-Claude protested, gallantly holding out his hand to help her up the last two steps.

At five feet ten inches and wearing heels, Gaby towered over the diminutive designer, but his short stature didn't keep him from being noticed in any crowd. His black hair slicked straight back from a high forehead, and his jaunty oversize handlebar mustache, which was his trademark, made people aware of Jean-Claude's presence the moment he entered a room.

When Raphael joined them on the deck, Jean-Claude urged, "Turn—let me see how the gown moves with you."

As she pirouetted the designer clapped his hands in delight. "My most perfect creation!"

Gaby glanced down at her gown, puzzled. It was beautiful, made of shimmering teal blue silk, elegantly draped, hinting at its Grecian inspiration, but it certainly wasn't the most perfect thing he'd ever designed. "Do you really think so? That gown you designed for last season's finale was a lot more—"

"No, no, *ma chérie*, you misunderstand. The gown, *oui*, it is beautiful. I design nothing less; yet, it is you who are my most perfect creation."

Jean-Claude puffed up his chest proudly as he turned to Raphael to explain. "Of all the French designers, only I was asked to come to America to show my collection at that Neiman-Marcus *magnifique* fortnight in Dallas. There I saw this creature walk out onto the runway, auditioning for a spot in the show. Gangly, unsure, like a frightened colt, and totally innocent to the aura she radiated, she stole my heart. A lady, I thought, yet a lady of fire," he said, echoing Raphael's words.

He pulled himself up to his full five feet six inches. "The fools—they didn't want to hire her; but I, Jean-Claude, have ways of getting what I want. When I demanded her name, they told me she was called Gaby O'Shea." He threw his hands up in the air. "*Gaby!* I ask you Raphael, *mon ami*, is that a proper name for a work of art?"

Before he could reply, the exuberant Jean-Claude charged on. "No, for me when I brought her to Paris, she had to become Gabrielle, a name fit for so beautiful a woman. And now the whole world knows her by that name."

Gaby hugged him. "Jean-Claude, call me Gabrielle if you wish, but remember, underneath all this glitter and polish you've given me, I still prefer cowboy boots to high heels, and long-neck beer to champagne." She glanced over his shoulder and winked at Raphael. "I could even swear I prefer the Dallas Cowboys to soccer . . . but I won't."

"Enough! You shatter my illusions," the designer scolded. "For me you will always be Gabrielle!" He fastidiously wrinkled his nose. "I shall never call you Gaby. Now come, you must go with me to meet Niko. Charm him, *ma chérie*. With my brilliant designs and your beauty we can't fail."

"I think I'll find the champagne while you two discuss business with our Greek host," Raphael commented, turning to leave them.

"No, no, you must join us," Jean-Claude urged. "Niko is a great soccer fan. He will want to meet you." Then, with typical Gallic common sense, he added in an undertone, "You can't play soccer forever. The legs, they will go. Remember, *mon ami*, Niko is a very powerful man. It would not hurt to befriend him. Who knows, someday you might do some business together."

With a casual shrug Raphael agreed. "You're right. I've met Niko before, but it won't hurt to renew that acquaintance. It's always nice to have a billionaire or two for a friend. But let's detour by the bar. The night is warm. Maybe some champagne will help cool me off."

"It didn't earlier this evening," Gaby teased pro-

27

vocatively as Jean-Claude bustled off ahead of them in search of their host.

Raphael's eyes darkened. "A few more words like that, saucy lady, and business or no business, I'm taking you back to the villa, the champagne, and the moonlight!"

"Okay," Gaby laughed, "I'll behave . . . for now."

Gaby's steps lagged as she gazed around her, drinking in all the surroundings. "This really is a fabulous yacht! I'd read about it, but it's even more incredible than words can describe. Maybe you should go into the oil-tanker business. Obviously it pays better than kicking a soccer ball."

"No doubt, but I don't think I'm cut out to be a businessman. Three-piece suits and boardrooms would bore me."

"Too confining, right?"

Raphael laughed as he tapped her gently on her forehead. "I knew I shouldn't have gotten involved with such a bright lady. You know me too well, don't you, Gabrielle? You know I hate traps of any kind."

Before she could reply, Jean-Claude called from the doorway of the salon, "Will you two hurry! The *amour*, it can wait till later."

Gaby and Raphael left the open deck and entered the spacious salon where most of the guests had gathered. A band was playing and couples were dancing as they made their way toward the rosewood bar where the champagne was being served. As they neared, Gaby's glance became enthralled by the large painting by Van Gogh hanging behind it. It was an exquisite picture, full of sunshine glittering brightly over a field of wild flowers all done in luminous shades of blue, green, and yellow. A

28

happy painting, it was obviously done before madness began to distort the artist's work.

Its impact was heightened because Niko had pulled colors from it to decorate the rest of the salon. The walls were covered with sea-green silk, and the barstools were upholstered with pale yellow leather; then, most beautiful of all, was the mosaic done in lapis lazuli on the dance floor.

She tugged on Raphael's arm to make him stop. "Isn't that floor breathtaking?" she whispered, discreetly pointing.

He shrugged. "I guess so, if you like leaping dolphins. Niko said it's copied from some ruins on Crete. During the day the roof slides back and the floor drops ten feet to become the bottom of a swimming pool. Last time I was here, we—"

"The last time you were here?" she asked, surprised. "I didn't know you'd partied with Niko before."

"Sure." He laughed. "That was during my bevy-of-women phase, but that's ancient history, as they say. Come on, my one and only, let's grab a couple of glasses of champagne, and then we'd better join Jean-Claude. It looks like he's cornered Niko."

Gaby glanced at him as they walked across the room to join the two men. Raphael's reputation as a playboy was well earned. She knew there had been women—a lot of other women—in his life before they'd met, but the thought of him in anyone else's arms still hurt. He said that he loved her, that she meant more to him than anyone he'd ever known. She prayed, for the safety of her own heart, that he was telling the truth, because her feelings for him were growing, multiplying, reaching so deeply within her, they were wrapping about her heart

29

with a power that thrilled . . . and it frightened her.

Her smile was a bit forced when they reached Niko and Jean-Claude. After exchanging greetings, the designer said, "Ah, Gabrielle, Niko has been most anxious to meet you and see my latest creation." He turned to the other man. "See, *mon ami,* the gown is as beautiful as I promised."

Their Greek host bowed gallantly over her hand. After brushing it with a kiss, he vowed, "Jean-Claude, you are undoubtedly a brilliant designer, but even you can't make a gown that can compete with Gabrielle's beauty. Raphael, you are a very lucky man." He sighed with exaggerated sadness. "If I were a bit younger and if my wife didn't have eyes as sharp as Hera's own, I'd try to win this lovely woman for myself."

Jean-Claude tapped his foot impatiently as Niko's compliments rolled on. Finally he interrupted, "I brought some other gowns with me. If you'd like Gabrielle to change so you can see more of the designs, I'm sure she wouldn't mind. . . ."

"No, no, that's unnecessary." Niko chuckled. "This is a party. Gabrielle is here to enjoy herself, not parade around as if this were your showroom in Paris."

"But, *mon ami,*" Jean-Claude protested, "you said we'd discuss backing my—"

Niko held up his hand to silence him. "Tonight of all nights is not the time to talk business. Besides, I don't need to be sold. I've seen your designs. Send the contract to my office in Athens." His hearty clap on Jean-Claude's shoulder made the smaller man totter. "And I guarantee we'll be successful. Whatever I touch on this special day will be blessed by the gods." He gestured imperiously to a passing

30

waiter to bring over his tray of champagne glasses. "Now, my friends, I must go. Fill your glasses, then raise them with me as I make a joyous announcement."

Curious, they watched Niko hurry across the room and murmur something to the man directing the band. Then, with a drum roll to gather everyone's attention, he walked to the center of the dance floor. He spread his arms wide as if to embrace the party. "My friends, tonight is a night of joy. We shall let the ouzo flow. We shall roll the ceiling back so the moonlight can smile down on us and bless this night. We shall dance, sing, and toast —" He paused, letting the curiosity build. "—and toast the engagement of my daughter, Phaedra, to Markos Damaskinos, the son of my great friend, Costis. Come Phaedra, Markos, let everyone see your happiness."

As Jean-Claude rushed forward to offer congratulations, Raphael muttered under his breath, "The fool!"

Surprised, Gaby's head snapped around. "Who's a fool, Phaedra or Markos?"

"Markos. Who else?" he insisted, downing his champagne in one gulp, then setting his glass aside.

Gaby glanced at the embracing couple, then looked back at Raphael. "I admit she's not the most gorgeous woman in the world, but you have to admit her dowry more than makes up for that. With Niko's wealth behind her she must be worth millions!"

"Millions or not, he's still a fool to trade his freedom for a wedding ring."

Gaby gazed at him a long time. Then, before she could stop the words, the question in her heart

31

slipped out. "And what would it take to make you give up your freedom?"

Raphael shook his head. "I don't know. Nothing has ever tempted me enough . . . not even being in love."

The way his voice caressed the word *love*, the way he looked at her when he said it, made her heart race. Yet, at the same time it hurt to have him admit he valued his freedom more than his love for her.

Could she ever make that love strong enough to bind him? The instant that thought flashed through her mind, Gaby quickly brushed it away. Raphael was like an eagle soaring free, and trying to force him to land, to remain at her side, might destroy them both. He was Spanish, with a fierce Latin pride. If they had a future—and with her every breath she prayed that they did—it had to be by Raphael's choice. She could not force him.

She swallowed back the lingering hurt and smiled up at him. "Hmmm, so you've never been tempted enough? What a challenge! I guess I'll just have to be more creative with the temptations I offer."

Raphael winked at her as he rubbed his hands together. "Sounds like we're in for some interesting times! And you can bet I'll be a willing victim. You've got a body that would tempt a saint." He chuckled roguishly as his hands began to stroke her bare arm suggestively. "And since I'm hardly a saint, as I said, it should be very interesting! When does all this temptation begin? Do I have time for another glass of champagne?"

"Sure, maybe even two." She linked her arm with his as they started back toward the bar. "I think I'll surprise you. That way you won't have time to throw up any defenses against my wicked ways."

"Wicked ways! This is sounding better and better all the time! You may win yet."

Dear God, I hope so! she silently prayed as they continued across the room.

Raphael took her empty glass, then handed her a fresh glass of the sparkling wine. "Niko had his toast, now I have one of my own, for I want this night to be as special for us as it is for him." He raised his glass to her. "To Gabrielle, may your wicked loving ways make tonight a night we'll never forget."

Gaby clinked her glass against his as she vowed from her heart, "I'll do my best!"

When both glasses were empty she ran her fingertips up his chest, not stopping until she could lock her fingers behind his powerful neck. "The band has switched from rock to something a lot slower, a lot sexier. Are you brave enough to try fending off some of my wicked ways on the dance floor?"

Raphael bent his dark head toward her until he could whisper in her ear. "If there weren't a hundred people milling around here, I'd lay you down on your back right now and teach you a few wicked ways of my own."

The embers of desire within her began to warm, then blaze, as his tongue darted into her ear, delivering its own message of desire before he continued. Her fingers twined in his thick hair as his final husky promise sent a shiver of delight trembling through her. "And you would enjoy them, my Gabrielle . . . every last one of them!"

He drew away so he could look down into her eyes. A small sigh escaped. "But unfortunately there are those hundred people, so for now I guess I'll have to be content to hold you against me on the

33

dance floor instead of underneath me in the moonlight back at the villa."

One of her fingertips reached up to trace his firm lips. When his lips parted she let it slip inside, reveling in the feel of the velvety softness of his tongue against her skin. "Isn't it wonderful that the moon will be shining for so many more hours tonight?"

Raphael's fingers closed over hers, drawing her hand away as he struggled to control his breathing. "Hundred people or no, if you keep touching me like that, we're going to skip the dance floor entirely and go right on to the main course."

"We couldn't have that, could we?" Gaby teased, moving out of his reach. "You should never skip the appetizer." She smiled at him with special meaning. "It always makes that 'main course' just that much more enjoyable. So let's dance."

"Maybe you're right," Raphael agreed, sweeping her into his embrace as the band began playing another love ballad. "I have a feeling tonight's 'dinner' is going to be something especially memorable, and I want to savor every moment of its creation."

Slowly the music began to weave its spell about them as they moved as one across the dance floor inlaid with the beautiful lapis lazuli. Lapis lazuli, gem of the gods, prized by the pharaohs, a special stone for this special night. As they danced its unique magic surrounded them like a satin cloak, insulating them from everything but pleasure.

Gaby's arms wound around Raphael's back, drawing him even closer against her body. Swaying to the music, she felt the firm power of his hard chest rippling against the softness of her breasts. She heard the words of love, of wanting, whispered in her ear, and answered with a silent message of her own as her hands explored his back, then tugged his

34

shirttail from his pants so they could slip beneath and find the warmth of his flesh.

"Let's go out on deck," he said softly, guiding her toward the door. "Privacy is a wonderful thing."

In the moonlight outside the salon they danced alone. The music, muted, more dreamy now, created a world around them in which feeling, touching, desiring, became their only reality. Each sensation he invoked within her spiraled outward through her body, heating, firing a wanting within her until every part of her ached with a longing only he could satisfy. As her lips moved against his throat she heard a low moan escape and she smiled, knowing the fire raged as hotly within him. Then, because she wanted that fire stoked even hotter, her kisses returned to taste of his flesh again.

The passionate throb of the music echoed their own rising need as their steps slowed until they were hardly moving. As Gaby deliberately arched her body against Raphael's, he leaned her back against the teak rail and nestled one heavily muscled leg between her thighs.

"Ah, that's unfair: You know I can't resist your legs," she sighed, enjoying the scandalous sensations triggered by the play of his hard thigh against her soft flesh.

"Who said seduction was supposed to be fair?" he murmured, burying his face in the scented cloud of her dark red hair.

"I thought I was supposed to use my wicked ways on you," she whispered in mock protest.

That pulled a husky chuckle from Raphael as he moved to let a shaft of moonlight between them. "Why not be wicked together?"

Then his smile faded as the desire within him

turned the black of his eyes into burning coals. "Come, Gabrielle, it is time."

They started toward the ladder that would take them to the waiting motor launch, then Raphael suddenly snapped his fingers and pulled her to a stop. "Wait, I forgot something."

"Yes, I agree." She nodded. "We did get a bit carried away and forgot our manners. We ought to say good-bye to Niko and Jean-Claude."

Raphael's arm tightened about her waist. "That's not exactly what I had in mind, but you're right. After all, it has been a great party."

The crowd in the salon had thinned so it wasn't difficult to spot the two men. As they neared they heard Niko insist, "Jean-Claude you must design Phaedra's wedding gown. I shall have no other. And we will have the wedding outside in the gardens of my villa."

When he caught their approach out of the corner of his eye, he turned to greet them. "Come join us; we are planning Phaedra's wedding. Of course, you both must plan to come. I insist. It'll be the wedding of the decade!" he bragged.

With his millions Gaby had no doubt it would be. She smiled. "I would love to come. Niko, it's been a wonderful party, but Raphael and I have to leave. Unfortunately, being a model, I do need my beauty sleep."

"Sure, I understand!"

The glitter in Niko's eyes told her he understood all too well what they were up to! He slapped Raphael on the back. "My friend, I have no doubt you *will* see she gets to bed."

Raphael leaned over to whisper a question to their host. Then Niko's hearty laugh reverberated off the walls. "Of course. Take as many as you want. Ah, to be young again!"

"What did you ask him?" Gaby demanded after she'd kissed Jean-Claude's cheek in farewell and they'd started across the room.

Raphael pulled her to a halt. His gaze raked slowly over her figure, lingering a breathless moment on her breasts thrusting against the teal silk; then he smiled, obviously in anticipation. "I asked him if I could take a bottle of champagne home with us." He spread his hands and shrugged. "Can you blame me? The moonlight, the sea breeze"—his voice dropped to a husky purr—"the thought of you lying naked—can I help it if it made me thirsty again!"

Maybe it was that anticipation or maybe it was all the champagne he'd drunk, but Raphael drove even faster than before over the narrow mountain roads as he turned his Alfa Romeo back toward the villa.

Gaby shut her eyes and said a silent prayer as they squealed around a corner on two wheels, then straightened out with a roar from the powerful motor. Nervously she grabbed the armrest, bracing for another curve. "Raphael, I—"

"I know," he laughed, one hand reaching out to stroke her hair, "I can't wait either. Maybe I should trade this sports car in for a van, but I don't think that's my style."

She wanted to beg him to put both hands on the wheel, but knew it would provoke another argument if she said anything. She forced herself to relax by reminding herself that Raphael was an excellent driver; otherwise he'd never have earned his FIAA license from the International Racing Federation, which had allowed him to race at Monte Carlo. Still, a long sigh of relief escaped when she saw the lights of the villa.

Raphael's teeth flashed against the darkness in a grin when he heard the sigh. "I know how you feel, my Gabrielle. I'm as anxious to get there as you are! The champagne is cold, I am not, and the moon will tell no secrets of the pleasures we exchange. It should be—

"Dios mío!" he shouted as the blinding lights of a huge truck loomed suddenly in front of them as they whizzed around the final curve. With a quick twist of his wrist he sent the car skidding to the right. The tires squealed in protest as they bit into the gravel on the shoulder of the road, tried to hold . . . but couldn't.

Gabrielle's scream shattered the silence of the night as the car careened through the guardrail and sailed into space.

The moonlight, once welcomed and romantic, now became a sinister harbinger of danger as it illuminated the rocks lurking beneath the cliff. Gaby screamed again and threw her hands in front of her face, not wanting to see the fate waiting for them below.

Seconds before they hit, Gaby felt Raphael's strong arms wrap tightly around her, trying to protect her as the rocks rushed up to meet them.

"Gabrielle, I'm sorry!"

Raphael's words, torn from his throat, were the last thing she heard before the sickening sound of metal hitting stone. Rending, tearing at the car, the impact was so powerful, it wrenched her out of his arms. Helpless, she was flung through the air like a rag doll before she finally hit the rocks . . . hit hard!

Battered, bruised, the breath wrenched out of

her, she felt as if she were wrapped in a blanket of pain made of a thousand needles. Weakly, Gaby tried to move, tried to escape the agony, then fell back gasping as a tremendous stab of pain, sharper than any she'd ever endured, seared her leg. The intensity of the pain stole the scream from her lips. Then it began to ebb as she felt a darkness starting to close in on her. She fought against it, fearing she would never awake, but slowly the darkness won.

Fading, like the picture flickering off the screen at the end of a movie—is this what it feels like to die? she wondered through the mists fogging her mind.

The shroud of blackness was almost complete when she heard Raphael's voice repeating over and over in an anguished chant, "Gabrielle, I'm sorry. . . . Gabrielle, I'm sorry. . . ."

Then she heard nothing.

Itching? That's a strange thing to feel in heaven. The thought vaguely floated through Gaby's muddled mind before she slipped back into the welcome darkness of unconsciousness, where there was no itching, no pain, no terrifying memories.

An hour later she stirred again. *Yes, my leg definitely itches!*

A tiny smile touched her lips, welcoming the uncomfortable sensation, for she knew God wouldn't allow anything as disagreeable as that to happen to his angels. Therefore she wasn't an angel! That triumphant conclusion helped sweep some of the fog from her thoughts, allowing voices to penetrate.

"Jean-Claude, did you see that! I think she's finally coming around. She moved!"

Raphael clutched the other man's arm so hard, he winced but he didn't protest. Instead he scolded, "Yes, *mon ami*, she did, even if you did your best to

39

see that she never moved again. How could you have been so stupid? You know how treacherous those mountain roads are. And don't try and tell me you weren't driving too fast: You don't drive any other way."

Jean-Claude's rage stirred Gaby. Even though every inch of her body ached, she had to protest. "Please," she whispered weakly, "it wasn't his fault."

With a delighted whoop Raphael leaned over the railing of her hospital bed so he could touch her. When he bent to kiss her gently, she felt the dampness of his tears touch her cheeks. "Gabrielle, you have come back to me. But, my love, don't defend me. Jean-Claude is right: The accident was my fault. I was driving too fast. Look at me," he begged. The intensity of the emotion he experienced cracked his voice. "Can you forgive me?"

Slowly, with effort, her eyelids fluttered open. She blinked, extending her hand toward him as she gasped, "Raphael, your face! You look . . ."

"I know. I look like I walked into someone's fist, but don't worry, it's just a black eye. It's tender but it's not serious."

As she struggled to move so she could touch his battered face, she felt a heavy weight dragging at her leg. Only then did she become aware of the plaster cast encasing her right leg from her ankle to her hip. With a trembling smile she admitted, "I knew angels didn't itch."

Before Raphael or Jean-Claude could demand an explanation for this odd statement, the doctor pushed open the door and entered her hospital room. In heavily accented English he observed, "Good, our sleeping beauty is finally awake."

"How long have I been out?" she asked, still

struggling to clear the last of the groggy mist from her thoughts.

"Five days," the doctor answered crisply as he put his fingers on her wrist, testing her pulse. "But if this heartbeat is to be believed, you're not much the worse for the ordeal."

"Not much the worse!" Jean-Claude raged at him. "She's covered with bruises, she has three cracked ribs, there's a cast covering one of her magnificent legs, and—"

"Calm down," the doctor soothed. "Remember, it could have been a lot more serious. Both of you were very lucky," the doctor said, looking first at Raphael and then at Gaby. "Ribs, a broken leg—they will heal."

"When?" the designer demanded. "I want to take Gabrielle with me to New York in August to launch my new signature line. Niko wants her to be the focus of the . . . Why are you shaking your head like that?" he demanded as the doctor interrupted him.

"Let me explain. Mademoiselle O'Shea's leg is broken in two places. The break of the fibula in the lower leg is not very serious; nor are the cracked ribs. They shouldn't take long to heal. However, she also broke the femur, the big bone in the thigh. And to make it worse, the break is near the hip joint. Now, it is my professional opinion that this break will take much longer to—"

Jean-Claude threw his hands in the air. "Will you stop with this medical double-talk and tell us how soon Gabrielle will be able to walk on the runway again. I need her."

Raphael leaned toward the bed and squeezed her hand. "I need you too." His smile did nothing to ease the concern shadowing his dark eyes.

41

The doctor glanced at Jean-Claude, then back down at Gaby. "No one can be sure how soon your bones will mend. However, I assure you, you will not be able to take that trip to New York in August. With a break of the femur this serious, you will have to be in a cast for an extended period of time. Then, even when the cast is removed, you will have to use crutches for a month or two." He paused, unable to meet Gaby's horrified gaze. "I don't believe in building up any false hopes, so I'm going to be blunt: Even with intense physical therapy, it may be nine months to a year before you can walk normally again without the use of a cane."

A year! That knowledge blasted away the last bit of fog slowing her thoughts. Feeling suddenly queasy, Gaby shut her eyes as if trying to deny the reality of what was happening to her. She did not see Raphael go pale under his dark tan when he heard the doctor's ominous prediction.

"A year!" he repeated her thoughts in a shocked whisper. Then he squared his shoulders. He looked at the other two men. "I want to be alone with Gabrielle. We must talk. There is much we must plan for the future."

Jean-Claude nodded in understanding. Then he bent to kiss Gaby's cheek. "A year, two years, it does not matter. You will always have a modeling job waiting for you in my showroom, *ma chérie*."

When they were alone in the room, Raphael began pacing. "I've had a lot of time to think over the last five days, and I have planned everything. After we're married, I'll take you back to Spain to meet my parents. You'll need time to recuperate, and their ranch near Barcelona will be the perfect place." He shoved an impatient hand through his hair. "They'll be delighted. They have been urging

42

me for years to take a wife and start delivering grandchildren." His lips twisted into a rueful grin. "I guess that project will have to wait until you're out of that cast. Let's pray your bones knit fast! Then, when soccer season starts . . ."

Gaby stared at him for a long moment, her heart breaking as she listened to his words. She'd dreamed so often that Raphael's love would grow strong enough that he couldn't live without her, that he'd eventually ask her to marry him, but not this way, not for these reasons . . . not because he felt guilty that he'd been driving the night of the accident. She didn't want to become his *responsibility!*

Finally she interrupted before the hurt could plunge any deeper. "Raphael, stop. Listen to yourself," she pleaded unhappily. "You're talking about our future, but you aren't showing any emotion. You're talking about making your parents happy, but you haven't said anything about yourself. And most importantly, you aren't talking about love. Love," she repeated, "that's why people marry. If that's not the real reason, it won't work."

"Gabrielle, you don't understand. I want to take care of you. Didn't you listen to what the doctor said? It will be at least nine months before you will be able to walk out on a runway again. How will you live?"

A sad smile touched her lips. "Not everyone is like you, Raphael. Not everyone spends every dime they make. You're always accusing me of being too conservative. This is one time I'm delighted I am. I've got plenty of money saved. I can take care of myself."

"But, Gabrielle, listen to me: I do love you. I told you that."

"You don't love me enough! Remember what you said at Niko's party? You said you hated traps, that you'd never trade your freedom for a wedding ring."

"Those were just foolish words, words I said after drinking too much champagne. Things have changed. I meant what I said. I want you to marry me. I want to take care of you. I promise—"

"Raphael it would never work. I know you better than any man I've ever known in my life. The things you said weren't foolish words. You spoke them from your heart." Hot tears blurred her eyes. "You're not ready to settle down and get married. I'm not sure you ever will be. And I'm not going to use this accident to trap you. Eventually you'd come to resent it and in turn resent me. I couldn't bear to watch what love you do have for me turn to hate. That would break my heart, and that's a break that would never heal."

"Gabrielle, I insist you listen to me!"

A tear trickled down her cheek. "I can't listen anymore. It hurts too much," she whispered as emotion threatened to choke her.

She loved him so much! Yet, she had no choice but to let him go. You can't tether an eagle without destroying it or it destroying you. In her heart she knew she'd never love another man the way she loved Raphael, but there were times when even love wasn't enough. This, tragically, was one of those times. The pain of realizing that burned through her heart, searing her soul, branding it with a scar she knew would last forever. Suddenly she couldn't stand to look at him when she said good-bye.

Turning her face to stare at the blank, sterile wall

of the hospital room, she whispered, "Raphael, go . . . please go. It's over."

"No it isn't!" he insisted, exasperation sharpening his voice. "After what you've gone through the last five days, you just aren't thinking clearly. But you're too weak to argue with right now. So I'm going to leave and let you rest. But I will be back." He moved to touch her; then his hand fell back to his side as he repeated, "It isn't over between us!"

Fresh tears gathered as Gaby turned her head to watch the door swing shut, closing Raphael out of her life.

Yes, Raphael, it is over. My good-bye was forever. It has to be. You won't marry me for love. I won't let you marry me out of pity. In the end it would destroy both of us.

"Think of me sometime, Raphael," she whispered across the empty room. "For I shall never forget you."

CHAPTER THREE

Gaby rubbed her tired eyes, then went back to flipping through the pages of another aspiring model's portfolio. She was just closing the book when her secretary, Margie, knocked, then came bursting into her office.

"More flowers!" Margie sighed, burying her face in the fragrant bouquet. "You sure have some ardent admirer! Now the only problem is figuring out where to put these," she commented, glancing from the two dozen yellow roses on the table under the picture window, to the spray of pink gladioli on the computer stand, to the vase of Texas bluebonnets on top of the filing cabinet, then finally to the tiny nosegay of violets on the corner of Gaby's cherry wood desk.

She looked back at her boss. "Well, what do you think? About the only open spot left is on top of the computer. Shall I put these, ah, these . . ." She paused, frowning, as she looked at the bouquet of tiny blue flowers in her hands. "What are these things, anyway? I've never seen flowers like these."

A smile of remembrance crossed Gaby's face. "That's because they're grown mostly in Europe. They're forget-me-nots."

Margie's hazel eyes sparkled with excitement. "Ooooh, that's even more romantic! Flowers sent all the way from Europe. Okay, Gabrielle, you know I'm dying of curiosity. Just *who* are you supposed not to forget?" she asked, handing the bouquet to Gaby.

As one fingertip traced over the delicate blooms Gaby confessed, "Honestly, I wish I knew. I'm as much in the fog about my mysterious admirer as you are."

Margie's lip curled in disbelief. "Sure you are! But I won't pester you. Just promise me one thing: Promise me you'll ask this guy if he has a brother. I'd love to have someone romancing me with hourly deliveries of flowers."

Her secretary waited expectantly, hoping Gaby would satisfy her burning curiosity, but instead Gaby shrugged it aside. "It's probably just some male model who's trying to woo me with flowers so my agency will sign him to an exclusive contract. And speaking of contracts, has the contract come in for the fall designer show at the Apparel Mart?"

"Sure. It came in this morning. Why did you even bother to ask? You knew you had that guy who's representing the mart completely snowed. I wish I had your touch. You just sit there, looking gorgeous, and men fall over themselves handing you contracts. Unfortunately my mousy brown hair doesn't have the same affect on men."

Gaby's blue eyes hardened to a glittering sapphire, and there was a sharp edge to her voice as she commented, "Margie, you're the best secretary I've ever had, but if you don't want your next address to be the unemployment line, you'd better keep your facts straight. No one 'hands' me contracts; I earn them. When I returned from France three years ago, the only thing I had was a busted leg and the name Gabrielle—a name that isn't even mine.

47

Since then I've slaved twelve hours a day or longer to build Gabrielle Presents into one of the strongest modeling agencies in Dallas. I get those contracts because I've worked my . . . because I've worked very hard to find new faces for my clients. Men don't hand me contracts because of the way I look! Got it?"

"Sure, sure. Don't get riled," Margie soothed, unfazed by Gaby's outburst. "I've got it. Now, what I'd like to get is the name of the guy who's sending all these pretty posies."

Gaby sighed in exasperation. If Margie weren't the only secretary she'd ever had who could take dictation at the rapid speed she gave it, she might . . . Oh, well, how could she blame Margie for being curious? She glanced at the forget-me-nots in her hand. She herself wondered who was sending all the flowers.

"When I find out, you'll be the first person I tell," Gaby promised. "Now, please go get your pad. I've got a lot of letters that need to go out concerning the fashion show we're doing for the wives at the dental convention."

After crisply dictating enough letters to keep Margie tied to her typewriter till closing, Gaby leaned back in her leather desk chair and stared at the bouquet of forget-me-nots. Who was the mystery man? she wondered, silently reviewing the list of men she'd been seeing. John, the ad executive, who flew in periodically from New York? Richard, Dallas's top male model, who was pushing hard to be at the top of her personal-favorites list? Maybe it was Hamilton, the VP at Republic Bank and Trust. Or it could be . . .

Slowly her thoughts turned in another direction. Forget-me-nots: flowers from Europe. She remembered them growing wild all over the Riviera. Could it be . . . No! Gaby slammed her fist down hard, stopping the thoughts.

I won't think about Raphael! she sternly ordered herself. *That part of my life is over.*

Deliberately redirecting her thoughts, she nodded to herself. She bet her mysterious admirer was Richard. Maybe all the flowers were his way of announcing he was ready to sign with her agency. Still, the nagging questions wouldn't go away. What if it wasn't Richard, or John, or Hamilton? What if Raphael . . .

"Damn it!" she muttered under her breath, shoving the forget-me-nots aside.

Wouldn't the past ever let her go? Raphael—he loomed like a specter, shadowing her days and, worse, haunting her nights. It had been three years since he'd walked out of that hospital room, and yet, the memories, the feelings, refused to fade. Even absent, he stopped her from finding happiness with any other man. She'd dated dozens since returning from France, but not one had even come close to sparking that special magic Raphael created within her.

"Damn him, damn him, damn him!" Her voice grated as fresh tears flooded her eyes. Wouldn't she ever be free of him, of the memories?

Abruptly she shoved the desk chair back and grabbed her briefcase. As she swept past, walking rapidly so Margie couldn't see her red eyes, she requested, "Call Frank and tell him I'm on the way. If anyone calls, I'll be at the Apparel Mart, checking on details for the designer show." Without waiting for any questions, she hurried out of the office.

The parking garage under her office building was dark and cool, a sharp contrast to the heat she knew was searing the late spring air outside. While she was whimsically contemplating the joy of moving her business to Alaska during the summer, a silver Mercedes slid to a stop at the curb next to her.

"Afternoon, Miss O'Shea. It's a scorcher out there, and it's only April! Think what August's going to be like," Frank commented as he held open the back door of the car for her.

As she carefully snapped her seatbelt closed, he asked in his soft Texas drawl, "Where to, ma'am?"

"The Apparel Mart. We've got a show to put on there in a couple of days."

The big car gathered speed on the ramp leading onto Stemmons Freeway. Frank commented, "Margie was telling me the other day that you used to be a model in Paris. If I may say so, you're so pretty, you ought to be having fun prancing around on the runway instead of toting that heavy brief-case."

She hesitated. "I find it more exciting to run a modeling business than to actually be a model. It's much more of a challenge, but thanks for the compliment."

Part of what she'd said was true. She loved the challenge of finding new talent, of coordinating the clothes and the accessories for a show, of bidding against a more established firm and walking away with the contract. She'd found the wheeling and dealing of swinging new deals, such as the contract she'd just gotten with the Apparel Mart, more exciting than anything she'd ever done in her life.

But that wasn't the sole reason she worked behind the scenes instead of on the stage. She guarded her secret carefully, so few people knew that occasionally she had to struggle out of bed in the morning and hobble about the room, working the stiff-

50

ness out of her leg. Or that her leg would sometimes lock on her, causing her to stumble. It wasn't serious, just inconvenient.

Gaby shook her head, tossing aside the unpleasant thoughts. Everything had worked out for the best. She was a lot more secure running her own agency than competing in the savage world of modeling, in which your "look" might be in one year and out the next. And besides the security, her success was finally beginning to add some plump padding to her savings account.

Suddenly a car swerved into the lane ahead of them. As Frank slammed on the brakes Gaby, sick with fear, squeezed her eyes tightly closed. Breathing hard, she tried to tell herself to relax, that the danger was over, but still her heart pounded. This unreasoning fear—the terror of cars, of driving, of having another accident—was the worst scar that lingered from the crash. The nightmares had lasted for months. Over and over she'd dreamed they were going over that cliff again, that the rocks were crouching like demons below her again, that the pain would rack her again. She'd wake, shaking, the sheets damp with her cold sweat.

And getting behind the wheel of a car was worse! She vividly remembered the first time she'd tried to drive after the accident. She couldn't stop trembling when her hands touched the steering wheel; then her fingers froze when she tried to turn the ignition key. No matter how hard she tried, she couldn't make herself start the car. She knew she was being ridiculous, but nothing could erase the trauma of what she'd experienced that awful night coming back from Niko's party.

Since it was virtually impossible to get around Dallas without a car, a friend who was a psychologist had finally suggested she try using a chauffeur, that maybe that would help. It had: Using a chauffeur and riding in a big car surrounded by a lot of strong metal had partly solved the problem. Now she never rode anywhere unless Frank was driving. Only that way could she cope with the horrible dread she felt each time she stepped into a car. Someday she knew she had to deal with this irrational phobia so she could go on with her life in a normal way. But not yet.

When Gaby had finalized all the details for the designer show at the Apparel Mart, she considered going back to the office, then decided she wanted to forget business for at least one evening. But she didn't find the peace her heart desperately needed. Instead, for the first time in a long time the nightmares of the crash returned to haunt her sleep.

She felt bleary-eyed the next morning as she pushed open the door to her suite of offices. Margie looked up from the magazine she was reading and smiled. "Sorry, boss, no more flowers. Your ardent admirer seems to be a little less ardent today. Sure you don't want to tell me who it is?"

Gaby shook her head and started for her private office. "Hey, wait a minute," Margie requested. "Didn't you tell me you used to model for Jean-Claude in Paris?"

"Yes. In fact, I'd probably still be with him if I hadn't decided it was time to leave Europe and come home. Why?"

"He's coming out with a line of men's sport clothing, and you should see the gorgeous hunk he's got representing the line!" She giggled, tapping the magazine. "He's a whole lot better-looking than any man who's ever walked through *our* door! Jim

52

Palmer, move over. American women have a new sex symbol!"

Gaby laughed at her secretary's enthusiasm. "Here, let me see that ad. I'm always willing to look at a gorgeous hunk. I can't think of a better way to start—"

Suddenly the words died as Gaby stared down at the picture. It featured a gleaming white yacht that looked startlingly like Niko's. A gathering of the "beautiful people" gazed adoringly at one man attired in a scarlet silk shirt unbuttoned to the waist. He had a sweater tossed casually over his shoulders, was wearing black linen slacks, and was drinking champagne. She swallowed back the tears as the memories raced back. It was a picture of Raphael.

As the magazine fell from her fingers, Margie jumped up from her chair. "Are you all right? You just went white as a sheet. Do you need some water? Shall I call a doctor? Do you want me to—"

Gaby interrupted the string of questions with a wave of her hand. "Margie, I'm fine. I guess the surprise startled me. I didn't expect to see someone I used to know starring in Jean-Claude's ad, that's all."

Reassured that her boss was all right, Margie's eyes eagerly returned to the advertisement. She gushed, "Ooooh, do you really know this fabulous creature? Will you introduce me? Hey, wait a minute. Is he your mysterious flower-sender?"

"No, he isn't!" Gaby flinched at the thought. "That's one thing I do know. I haven't seen him in three years. Besides, Raphael lives in Europe."

"Raphael," Margie sighed. "What a romantic name! Look, there's lots more pictures. Jean-Claude took out a four-page spread to launch his new men's

53

line," Margie explained, flipping the pages to show Gaby.

Raphael laughing, leaning back in a limousine, again drinking champagne, while a beautiful woman draped adoring arms around him. Raphael driving a red Ferrari with a voluptuous blonde at his side. Raphael pictured at the controls, flying a private jet this time with a redhead for a co-pilot.

Oh, great, this is just what I need: Raphael gazing up at me every time I pick up a magazine, Gaby thought, knowing she should close the magazine but somehow unable to draw herself away.

"It says here that your friend was chosen by Jean-Claude as the perfect image for his new line, and since he has retired from playing soccer, he will be active in promoting it." Margie glanced at her. "Gaby did you hear me? You seem a million miles away."

"No, just several thousand," she murmured, letting her thoughts drift backward to the time they spent together in Europe.

"Do you suppose he'll come to America?"

Gaby firmly shut the magazine. "Why should he when the champagne, the yachts, and the hordes of women obviously eager to drape themselves all over him are in Europe?"

"You sound a little bitter. I don't mean to pry, but if talking about it would—"

"No, Margie, I don't want to talk about it, and I am not bitter. Sometimes things just aren't meant to work out." Gaby turned toward her office, ending the discussion but unfortunately not ending her memories.

She tried to work—she needed to make the final selections on the models for the designer show—but she couldn't concentrate as the pictures in the

54

ad kept flashing through her mind. Raphael among the beautiful people—nothing had changed. She hadn't seen him in three years, but that didn't mean she hadn't known what he'd been doing. The fashion magazines, which she read as part of her business, always covered the comings and goings of the international jet set. She'd seen pictures of Raphael at a bash Niko threw to celebrate the birth of his first grandchild. That time he'd been with some blonde from Germany. Later it had been pictures of him skiing at Saint Moritz with a Scandinavian beauty. Then sailing in the Aegean with . . .

"Oh, hell!" Gaby muttered, putting a brake on the thoughts. "Why should I care who he's romancing this week?"

But unfortunately for the peace of her heart, she did care, and there didn't seem to be anything she could do to stop. Work—that was the only therapy, and for the next two days she threw herself so frantically into preparations for the designer show that when she returned to her lonely condominium, she was too tired to think . . . to remember . . . to miss. The only thing brightening her days were the daily deliveries of more flowers. Daisies, primroses, gardenias—they continued to arrive. Each day the flowers were different, except each afternoon the delivery ended with a bouquet of forget-me-nots. And still, the only thing on the card accompanying the flowers was her name.

On the afternoon of the rehearsal for the designer show, Gaby was backstage at the Apparel Mart, making a final check of her models' first change. She clapped her hands to get their attention. When their chatter died down she said, "You can tell from what you've got on that the jungle look is big in the couture market this year, so I've

55

selected some primitive music for this first part of the show. I want you to feel the music, to move with it. Be free. Be a little wild. Match your movements to the clothes. The buyers will love it! This run-through we'll try without my commentary so you can hear the music better," she suggested, waving to Margie to start the music.

As the muffled throb of jungle drums filled the air around them, Gaby checked each model closely to make sure every garment hung perfectly and that every accessory worked effectively. Only then did she let them through the curtain onto the runway that stretched out through the Great Hall.

"Wait a minute, Stephanie," Gaby ordered one of the last models in the line. "Your hem's uneven. Let me see if I can fix it. If not, we'll have to call the seamstress," she commented, dropping to her knees.

She was tugging on the fabric, trying to straighten it, when she felt someone sweep her long hair aside. Before she could react, warm lips began a sensual dance across the nape of her neck. Gaby's eyes closed as a sudden wave of weakness swept over her. So familiar, so powerful in their power to drug her senses, the kisses sent intoxicating ripples flowing outward, warming her blood, making her so light-headed, she almost felt as if she'd sipped a bit too much champagne. It couldn't be, yet she knew it was. No man but Raphael could make her feel such passion, such blazing need, with only his kiss.

"Ah, my Gabrielle," Raphael whispered in her ear, "no other woman in the world has hair the color of yours. How I have missed it. How I have missed you!"

Gaby twisted her head to look up at him; then she blinked, wondering if her dreams, her unrelieved need, had created an illusion. But no: Raphael was very real as he smiled his special smile just for her. "Aren't you going to get up off your knees and *properly* welcome me to Dallas?"

Stephanie, wide-eyed at what was happening in front of her, recalled Gaby to her senses when she observed, "Obviously I'm ruining one helluva reunion. I'll have someone else fix this hem." She giggled. "You've got better things to do!" Before Gaby could say anything she hurried off.

"Well, my Gabrielle, are you going to stay down on that floor forever?"

The soft Spanish accent caressing his words sent new chills through Gaby as she started to rise. Suddenly, as it sometimes did, her leg locked and she couldn't move. A stab of embarrassment shot through her as she mumbled, "Raphael, you're going to have to help me up. I'm stuck."

With a firm hand under her elbow he helped her to her feet. When her gaze met his she saw the guilt saddening his eyes as he admitted, "I did that to you, didn't I?"

"Don't look at me that way! Please don't!" she begged, hot tears threatening to scald her eyes. "I didn't want your pity three years ago, and I don't want it now. Besides, it's nothing serious. It doesn't happen very often, so you can save your pity for someone who needs it."

"It's not pity I feel when I look at you. I feel . . ." Raphael's hand clenched. "Oh, hell, this isn't how I wanted our reunion to be!"

"I don't want any kind of reunion at all!" she retorted, trying to convince herself as much as him.

Warm hands came up to cup her cheeks. "Gabrielle, you don't mean that. You can't fool me. Your lips may lie, but the truth shines in your eyes.

57

You want this to happen as much as I do. That's why I planned everything so carefully. The flowers . . ."

Somehow, deep in her heart, she wasn't surprised; still, she asked, "You mean *you*'ve been sending all those beautiful flowers?"

"Of course! Who else would send you forget-me-nots?" Suddenly his dark eyes flashed as a streak of jealousy flared and he moved a step back from her. "Or do you have so many lovers you can't sort them out?"

Refusing to admit that while there were men in her life, there was no man special enough to become her lover, Gaby retaliated, "You have no right to ask that, especially after you've been romping all over Europe with who knows how many women! I've seen your picture in the magazines. Skiing in Saint Moritz. Sailing in the Aegean. Dancing and drinking champagne at Niko's party. Attending the races at Ascot with—"

"Gabrielle, it's not what you think!" Raphael's voice dropped to a husky purr. "We must talk. There is so much I must tell you. So much has happened."

Even through her hurt, her irritation, Raphael reached out to her as no other man ever had. He wasn't even touching her, and yet, he could send her pulse skidding with just a look. His power was so compelling, Gaby felt herself weakening. What would it be like to kiss him again, to part his lips, to taste again the essence unique only to him? What would it be like to let those kisses build the desire until she lay beneath him, savoring the explosion of passion only his caresses could ignite? No, not again! her heart pleaded. Raphael had hurt her once, but slowly she'd recovered and started living again.

Letting herself feel for him spelled danger, a danger she might not survive this time.

As the silence stretched he pleaded, "Say something, Gabrielle. Say you will come talk with me."

Gaby gazed at him, remembering the past. Raphael hadn't changed. They had had no future three years ago. They had no future now, except possibly to resume their love affair. But passion was no longer enough for her. However, even as those thoughts filled her mind, desire to be in his arms filled her body. She had to protect herself. There was no other way.

She shook her head. "Raphael, we said all there was to say three years ago. I told you then it was over. It still is."

His hand shot out to grasp her arm. "And I told you it wasn't. And it isn't!"

Suddenly, Gaby realized they were attracting a lot of unwanted attention from the models returning backstage from their practice trip down the runway. She tugged her arm free and turned toward them. "Margie's out onstage, checking the lights. Stephanie, why don't you go ask her to get coffee for everyone." Then she spoke to the rest of them. "You can take a ten-minute break—in the dressing room." Her voice rose a notch to emphasize the last three words before she added, "After that, please change into the wool collection. We've got a lot of work to finish this afternoon."

When they were alone, Raphael moved to take her in his arms, but she backed away. "I thought you wanted to talk."

"We can talk later," he suggested with a rakish grin. "When I look at you, other things seem to take priority," he admitted, taking another step toward her.

59

Gaby knew that if he kissed her, held her in his arms, she'd be lost. Nothing would stop him from ending up in her bed. Her hands came up against his chest to hold him off. "We've got ten minutes before I have to get back to work, so if you have something you want to say, you'd better say it."

"Ten minutes to talk about three years. Gabrielle, I want to spend hours with you. See me tonight." Raphael's white teeth flashed, but his eyes looked a little sad. "After all, you never did deliver on your promise to tempt me with your wicked ways."

"No, I didn't, and I'm not going to!" Gaby insisted, bravely meeting his gaze even though just being near him was making her tremble inside.

"Too bad." Raphael sighed dramatically. "My resistance has weakened a lot since our visit to that villa in Saint-Tropez."

"Well, mine hasn't!" Gaby lied.

His hands reached up to take hers, trapping them against the warmth of his chest, making her feel again the smooth rippling of muscle as he breathed. "Are you sure? Or is the truth that you're afraid to be alone with me, afraid of how the evening might end?"

"No, that's not it at all!" she exclaimed, trying to free her hands from the disturbing sensations. He wouldn't let her go. "It's, ah . . . it's the fashion show I'm trying to put together. I'll be working till all hours."

"I'll wait," he said, firmly overriding her flimsy excuse. "Can't we at least talk as friends?"

"Friends? You've never been just friends with any woman!"

"No, I haven't, and I don't want to be just friends with you. But, my Gabrielle, if that's all you'll give me right now, I'll take it." His fingers twined with hers. "Can't you believe my intentions are honorable? They are, you know. Too bad we aren't in Spain: I'd even let you take along a duenna to protect you, just to prove it."

"I don't need protection from you or any man!" The emotions crackling through her sharpened her voice.

He misunderstood the tone as he observed, "You've changed, Gabrielle. You've grown so coolly efficient. Is there still a woman inside, or merely a business executive? Let me kiss you, let me hold you, let me find that woman I knew in France." His voice caressed the words as he spoke. "I know she's still there, waiting for me, wanting me as much as I want her."

The intensity of her reaction to what he had said made her feel as though he'd reached out and stoked a fire in her flesh. He called her cool. How wrong he was! Right now she was hot, hot with the need to melt in his arms and forget everything but finding him again. The ease with which he could manipulate her emotions frightened her.

Desperately she tried to pull the armor back around her. "Yes, I may have changed, but it's obvious you haven't! And that leaves us right where we were when—"

His grasp tightened around her fingers, making her wince. "Don't say that. I *have* changed!"

"Sure!"

"Don't push me, Gabrielle, or models or no models, I'll show you how much right here." Suddenly he shut his eyes as a deep frown furrowed his forehead. The fire had died in his gaze when he looked at her again. "Gabrielle, forgive me. I promised myself I wouldn't lose my temper. But you always did manage to get under my skin. Please, go out

61

with me tonight. Three years is a long time. Truly, I have changed. Let me show you. Let us dine, talk, recover the time we've lost."

When she didn't say anything, he all too clearly read her thoughts. "Don't you trust me? Is that why you wouldn't let me see you again at the hospital and returned all my letters unopened?" He paused, studying her intently as if trying to see into her soul. "Or, my Gabrielle, is it yourself you don't trust when we're together?"

That was a question she didn't want to answer, even to herself. And it certainly didn't help being so near to him, to have the throbbing of his heart beneath her palms, to have his hands caressing hers. Maybe being on the other side of a dinner table would be safer.

With a sigh she surrendered. "All right, Raphael. I suppose I have to eat anyway."

A wide grin split his face. "Good. I knew eventually you couldn't resist me. I'll pick you up at—"

"No!" Gaby interrupted quickly. "I'll meet you. Just tell me what time and where."

Obviously confused and hurt at her reluctance to ride with him, he stared down at her, then shrugged. "I guess the important thing is, you've finally agreed to be with me tonight."

"I've agreed to have dinner with you tonight," she corrected quickly.

He ignored her protest as he continued: "A candlelight dinner, champagne, then back to my apartment for brandy on the terrace." Desire sparked the black depths of his eyes. "Isn't it wonderful that the moonlight is as beautiful in Dallas as it was at our villa? Remember how it was that night, Gabrielle?"

"No, I don't!"

His laugh echoed through the empty wings. "Gabrielle, you can't lie. I can see your soul reflected in those gorgeous azure eyes of yours." He chuckled again. "Besides, your blush would rival a sunset. No, you remember that night, the heat of our passion, as well as I do."

If he could ignore her words, she could do the same. "Apartment?" she asked, skipping over the last of what he'd said. "That sounds like you're staying in Dallas."

That thought half thrilled her and half frightened her as he nodded. "I am—permanently. That's part of what I want to talk to you about tonight. You won't believe what has happened to me in the last six months since I quit playing soccer. Niko has agreed to—"

"Hey, Raphael, ol' pal, I've got everything fixed up just like we wanted it," a man called from the other wing.

When Raphael turned to frown at him, Gaby was finally able to pull her hands free.

"Fabian, not now. I'm busy." Raphael's commanding tone would have stopped most people, but not the man approaching them.

Fabian ran on as if Raphael hadn't even spoken. "Wait till you see who I've got lined up." He turned his head to call over his shoulder. "All right, girls, come on over. He can't wait to meet you."

Gaby's eyes narrowed to slits as three models, whom she recognized from another agency, draped themselves like clinging vines over Raphael. They smiled adoringly at him, totally ignoring her. Gaby couldn't decide whom she disliked most: the women, who acted as if she were invisible, or Fabian, whose brash accent and loud sport jacket of red and black buffalo plaid offended her.

Raphael lifted one of the clinging arms from around his neck as if he were trying to disengage a leech and insisted, "No, not tonight, Fabian!" His gaze never wavered from Gaby's face. "I told you, I've got other plans."

"Sorry, pal, everything's set, just like we planned. Dinner at the Mansion, dancing at Raffles, champagne at dawn—now, how can you disappoint these beautiful ladies when I've promised them all that and Raphael Salvaje besides."

"Just like we *planned!"* Gaby repeated to herself. She looked at him, anger tightening her mouth. Raphael with beautiful women clinging to each arm —it was just like all those pictures she'd seen in the magazines over the past three years.

Gaby's eyes shot hot sparks as she challenged him. "Time passes, but obviously nothing changes! Enjoy your dinner . . . and your companions. I've got a fashion show to produce," she said curtly, turning away.

"Gabrielle, wait!" Raphael pleaded. "Listen to me. It's my job!"

"Sure!" she muttered under her breath, not stopping. "I'll believe that when I believe a snowball won't melt in hell!"

CHAPTER FOUR

As Gaby walked away from Raphael, refusing to look back even when he called her name, her emotions felt as though they'd been twisted and pulled like a piece of taffy. Shock at Raphael's unexpected reappearance in her life battled with the anger she felt when she thought of him planning a cozy dinner for four—himself and three beautiful women. Yet, as powerfully as those feelings churned within her, they were overwhelmed and blunted by the desire still simmering in her blood, a reaction to his kiss, his touch. Tears scalded her eyes as she realized it was a reaction she had no ability to control.

Somehow she made it through the rest of the rehearsal; then with a headache throbbing violently between her temples, she directed Frank to take her home. Usually the serenity of the cool peaches and blues of her living room soothed her. Tonight not even they could help. With an exasperated oath Gaby poured herself a glass of iced tea, then walked out onto her patio. The searing heat of the day had eased up a little. Still, the air was sultry, but it wasn't the humidity that drove her back inside. No, the culprit was the moon. Shining full and round, it caught her up in the web of painful memories, memories of another moon, another night. They were memories she was desperately trying to forget but couldn't. With an angry yank she pulled the drapes closed over the French doors, then curled up in a miserable ball on the chintz-covered sofa.

What had she told Raphael? Time passes but nothing changes. How painfully true that was . . . for both of them. Raphael still made her feel every emotion a thousand times stronger than any other man who had ever touched her. Yet, three years had passed, and he still could not give her anything but passion—a passion she knew was no longer enough. Gaby didn't delude herself. She had enjoyed the blazing heat of their affair, the glamour, the parties with the jet set, just as much as Raphael had. But her Texas roots ran deep, and they had finally reached up to pull her back to reality.

Gaby took a sip of the iced tea, reflecting on her words. Then she shook her head. What she'd told Raphael wasn't completely true. True, he hadn't changed, but she had. While she was recuperating from the accident she'd had a lot of time to think, to evaluate what was really important in her life. She'd matured and now knew the value of substance over the superficial glitter of the type of life she'd lived in Europe. That was why she was running a modeling agency instead of just being a model. She'd learned something else about herself during all those months in the cast. Yes, she wanted fun, but she wanted that fun backed with security. And she'd learned that while she wanted passion, she wanted that passion made sweeter with commitment. And Raphael had always fought ties like that. So where did that leave them? Nowhere! That was where.

Gaby put her glass down on a coaster and stood up, secure in the logic of her thoughts. Yet, when she walked into her bedroom and saw the shimmering moon reflected in the mirror, she trembled.

Gaby flopped over onto her stomach and pulled the pillow over her head. The illuminated alarm clock read six thirty. "I've got to stop drinking so much tea. My dreams just get weirder and weirder," she muttered, closing her eyes. "Dreaming about someone hanging a picture at this hour is ridiculous!"

She was so exhausted, sleep grabbed her quickly. Only it didn't last. "Great!" she mumbled, stirring awake again. "This time it's a carillon chiming in my dream. How can I sleep with all this noise going on in my head?" After fluffing up her pillow, she laid her head down. But the pounding came again, followed by the ringing of her doorbell.

"So that's why my dreams are so noisy!" Gaby pulled on the silk robe matching her nightgown and started for the front door.

Raphael was leaning against the doorjamb when she opened the door. "I never knew you were such a sound sleeper. I've been ringing your doorbell and pounding for fifteen minutes. It's a wonder the neighbors didn't call the police. Gabrielle, we have to talk."

His gaze flickered over her as he walked into her living room. The sheer silk and lace of the negligee hinted at her figure rather than blatantly revealed it, but the effect was still arousing. Gaby pulled the sash a little tighter, uncomfortable with the hunger she saw burning in Raphael's black eyes . . . and her own immediate response to it.

He grinned at her. "If you greet all your callers like this, it's a wonder you get any sleep at all."

"It's six thirty in the morning, Raphael. What are you doing here?"

"I know it's early, but I couldn't wait any longer to see you."

"What do you want?"

"What do I want?" He raised an amused eyebrow. "What an opening!"

It had taken hours for her to go to sleep, hours during which desire had battled her resolution. The exhaustion had taken its toll, and she sank wearily down on the sofa. Her voice was a shade sharp as she complained, "Look, Raphael, I'm too tired to trade one-liners with you."

He stood for a moment, his hands on his hips, just looking at her. For breathless moments the air around them crackled with the magical intensity she always felt when he was near. It didn't get any easier for her to breathe when he settled down on the sofa next to her and started fiddling with her long hair.

"So you're tired," he repeated, a husky thread of longing deepening his voice. "Want me to put you to bed? After last night I can't think of anything I'd enjoy more."

" 'After last night,' " she mimicked. "I'm surprised you have energy left to carry me to bed. By the way, how did things go with your private harem?"

"Now hold it right there, Gabrielle. I don't have any harem, private or otherwise. That's the first thing we're going to get settled." He paused to rub his forehead. "But before we get into that, I need either an aspirin or a cup of coffee. I've got a splitting headache."

She patted his arm with mock concern. "Ah, poor Raphael. Were three women too much for you?"

"Gabrielle, for someone who professes not to care, your jealous claws are certainly sharp."

Refusing to admit how much it hurt to see him surrounded by other women, she lied. "I'm not jealous. I question your taste, that's all. I always thought you were a quality-before-quantity man. But maybe I misjudged you: Maybe you *have* changed."

Gaby expected to goad him into an angry retort. Fighting with Raphael was a whole lot safer than letting his nearness impel her toward him as it was doing right now.

But instead of snapping in anger, his voice remained surprisingly soft as his hand reached around to caress the back of her neck. "Gabrielle, I have missed you, missed your fire. Even spitting like a wildcat, you're still the most exquisite woman I've ever known. I promised myself I'd be the perfect gentleman this morning, but *Dios mío*, when I look at you, I'm lost. You would excite the Sphinx!"

Neither of them was breathing quite steadily as their gazes tangled. Finally, Gaby swallowed, breaking the spell. "Where are my manners? I believe you said you need an aspirin or some coffee."

"That's not all I need, Gabrielle."

She ignored his comment as she jumped up from the sofa. "I'm afraid all the aspirin's at the office. You'll have to settle for coffee," she explained, hurrying toward the kitchen.

In the kitchen she opened the cupboard where she kept the coffeepot. Suddenly her hand froze as she reached toward it. Why had she been so catty about his evening plans? She prided herself on being a lady; yet, the thought of him with another woman, or worse, three other women, turned her into a shrew. She shook her head. With Raphael around, none of her reactions made sense. He

69

threw her off balance and she didn't like it. Or maybe she liked it too much and that was what upset her. Again logic ordered her to shift her feelings into neutral and not feel anything for Raphael. Her heart scoffed, knowing that was impossible.

With a gasp she jumped when two hands, closing around her waist, broke through her reverie. "I came to find out if you'd fallen asleep on the way to the coffeepot," Raphael explained, letting his hands stroke the front of her silk robe.

"Raphael, don't!"

"Ah, yes." He chuckled. "What memories that phrase brings back! Got any champagne?"

"No, I don't!" Gaby paused as the same memories he spoke of flooded back to enthrall her emotions. Then abruptly she shut them off. The past was gone. Let memories be all that remains, she reminded herself as she continued. "Besides I thought you wanted coffee," she countered bringing the pot down to the counter. "Better let go: I can't reach the mugs from here."

Raphael's hands didn't move. The heat flowing from him into her did disturbing things to her heartbeat as he commented, "Maybe I'd better skip the coffee. Touching you again is enough stimulation for any man to handle."

"No, you wanted coffee, and that's what you're going to get. Besides, with luck it will get rid of your headache, you'll leave, and I can go back to bed," she joked. "I'm not due at the office until nine."

That's right, keep it light, Gaby ordered herself. *Then maybe you won't feel like tossing all caution out the door when he looks at you.*

"I'm willing to skip the coffee and head right for bed, if that's what you want," he suggested, starting to nibble on the back of her neck.

70

"Raphael, don't!" Gaby stopped herself. That was one phrase she'd definitely have to stop using! She started again. "I mean, I thought you wanted to talk. You can't talk and nibble at the same time."

"I don't suppose you'd settle for just the nibbling, would you?"

"No!"

"All right," he agreed as his hands dropped away from her waist. "I did pledge to be the complete gentleman. But, Gabrielle, I warn you, that's not going to be the case forever."

The heat throbbing through his promise warmed her like a strong gulp of the coffee she was pouring into the mugs. She did not turn to hand him his drink until she knew the flush had faded from her face.

When they were settled back in her living room, she said, "You get dinner at the Mansion, dancing at the hottest new spot in town, and lucky me, I get stuck going through a stack of portfolios, looking for a face with some character in it. I wish the models would go to college and learn something instead of trying to pull a Brooke Shields and make it to the top as teenagers."

"I know what you mean. Those three I took out last night didn't have a brain between them. Ego, yes, in spades; but none could string two intelligent sentences together."

Gaby patted his arm again. "Poor Raphael, having to suffer like that. I guess that's what comes with being America's latest sex symbol."

"What!"

She laughed. "At least, that's what my secretary thinks. She saw that ad layout you did for Jean-Claude and said you're a gorgeous hunk."

"And what do you think, Gabrielle?"

"I think . . ." She paused, teasing him. "I think in no time you'll have hordes of women chasing you. Isn't that what every man wants?"

Instead of laughing, his black eyes glowed hotly as he set his mug down on the coffee table. "Not this man! I don't want hordes of women. I want one— the one I am with right now. And I promise you, I *always* get what I want."

Her heartbeat skidded at the intensity she felt radiating out from him, touching her, trying to draw her to him; but that couldn't be. "Maybe not this time," she challenged. "Raphael, I meant what I said in France. It's over!"

"Keep telling yourself that. You might even convince yourself for a time. But you'll *never* convince me. It isn't over. Someday, somehow, you'll be mine again. I could have lived anywhere in the world, yet I chose to come to Dallas. Why do you think I moved here if not to find you, if not to hold you in my arms again?"

"Raphael, we're talking in circles," Gaby insisted, desperately trying to change the direction of the conversation before his words made her believe. "I say no. You say yes. It's time for me to get dressed. I've got a busy day ahead of me. Can't we finish this argument another time?"

"No, we can't." Raphael lifted the mug from her hands and set it aside. Before she could move, his fingers had entwined with hers, trapping her hands. "I don't care how busy you are today—I'm not letting another minute pass without explaining about what happened last night."

"You mean about you and your three dates? Believe me, I couldn't care less who or how many women you see. I'm free and so are you." Gaby shrugged casually. "Although I did think about you

72

dining at the Mansion when I heated up my leftover meat loaf. I'm just sorry the evening gave you a headache. But overindulgence will do that to you."

"Damn it, Gabrielle, will you stop chattering so I can explain!" The vehemence in Raphael's tone silenced her. "First, they were not dates—at least not dates the way you mean. As I tried to tell you, going out last night was part of my job. Fabian arranged everything. I'd never even met those models before. And don't look at me like that: I'm telling you the truth."

"You always did value the 'good' life. Three escorts, dinner at the poshest restaurant in town— what a dream job for you!"

Finally he smiled. "Well, I do have to admit, there are nice benefits. I've got a penthouse apartment in Turtle Creek and a Ferrari, so you can see why I couldn't turn it down when Niko called and—"

"Niko?" Gaby interrupted. "I thought you were working for Jean-Claude."

"I guess you could say I work for both of them. Jean-Claude created the men's line, and Niko agreed to back it, the way he's doing his signature line. Then, when Niko heard I'd retired from the soccer circuit, he came up with the idea of promoting it using me." A shadow crossed Raphael's features. "Needless to say, after Saint-Tropez, Jean-Claude wasn't exactly thrilled to have me as part of the deal, but Niko insisted."

Gaby hesitated, unhappy at the next question. "And just where do the women come into it?"

"It's all Madison Avenue hype. I'm the symbol. I'm supposed to live the good life, to dine at the best places, attract publicity, and so on. You know the gimmick: Wear Jean-Claude's designs and gorgeous women, fast cars, and wealth will all be yours."

73

"Not a bad job, if you can get it."

"No, especially not when the offer gave me a chance to find you again."

Gaby blinked, uncertain what he meant. Before she could ask, he continued, "It's simple. After you disappeared from my life, I figured if anyone knew where you had gone, it would be Jean-Claude. So I refused to sign the contract until he told me."

"I knew I shouldn't have ordered those negligees from him."

His gaze swept over her again, lingering a long breathless moment on the soft thrust of her breasts. Then he smiled. "I'm glad you did, for several reasons." His smile faded. "Please, Gabrielle, I don't want you to blame Jean-Claude. He protected your secret as long as he could, but Niko and I had him up against the wall. Niko made it clear the money was available only if I represented the line, and I wouldn't agree without your address."

She shrugged, trying to convince herself deep in her heart that she wasn't delighted Jean-Claude had betrayed her. "I guess it's too late for regrets now." She cocked her head and looked him over. "Tell me, why was Niko so insistent? Not that you aren't a gorgeous hunk, as my secretary describes you," she teased, "but a dozen other men might do just as well."

"I really don't know. One day he and Phaedra went into a huddle and he came out with this belief that I could sell the line better than anyone else."

"It's probably the name. I told you, Raphael Salvaje—Raphael the Savage—was irresistible to women."

"If that's true, how come we're sitting here, talking in the living room with coffee, instead of in the

74

bedroom with a bottle of champagne, which is where I really want to be?"

The thought of champagne, low lights, Raphael beside her in bed, stirred desires Gaby desperately wanted to ignore. She tried to joke, hoping he'd stop looking at her with such longing. "I guess I'm immune. Knowing you is like having chicken pox: Once you've had it, you can't get it again."

Raphael threw up his hands. "Oh, great, now you're comparing me to a disease. I think I'd like to meet your secretary. My ego needs some immediate repair work." Then a slow smile touched his face. "On the other hand, an easy conquest, like hurried lovemaking, never gives as great a pleasure. And as you remember, I can be a very patient lover. So take your time, Gabrielle; fight as much as you wish. We will both enjoy your surrender all the more."

She started to tell him in no uncertain terms that *surrender* wasn't in her vocabulary, when the doorbell rang. She glanced at her watch. "Good heavens, it's not even eight o'clock. Who would be ringing my doorbell so early?"

"Whoever it is, tell them to go away! This time is ours. I want to share you with no one."

"Raphael, shhh!" Gaby requested, unlocking the door. Her secretary was standing outside.

"Hi, boss, sorry to barge in so early but—"

Suddenly, Margie's words failed when she got a glimpse of Raphael standing in the middle of the room. Gaby laughed as her hazel eyes widened in startled wonder. "You *are* real," Margie whispered.

"Margie, stop gawking." Gaby turned to him. "Needless to say, this is my secretary. You remember, the one who thinks you're a gorgeous hunk."

Raphael smiled at Margie. "I'm charmed." Then,

bowing low over her hand, he kissed it with a continental flourish.

"Ooooooh." Beyond that, Margie was speechless.

"You never kissed *my* hand like that," Gaby protested with a laugh.

"Ah, no, with you I kissed other things. Remember?"

Gaby tossed a warning frown at him before looking back at her secretary, who still couldn't take her eyes off Raphael. Finally, in exasperation Gaby snapped her fingers in front of her secretary's eyes. "Margie, remember me? I'm the one who signs your paycheck every week. Care to tell me why you are here so early?"

Margie shook her head as if trying to clear it. Only then did she seem to be aware that Gaby was alone with Raphael in her nightgown. "Obviously, I should have called before coming. I'm sorry if I interrupted anything *interesting.*"

"Don't worry, you didn't interrupt anything important. We were just talking."

"Hmmmm." Margie's skeptical smile said she didn't believe a word of that nonsense. "The truth is, I couldn't call because your phone's been busy since last night. Either you've been having one heck of a conversation or it's off the hook."

Gaby glanced guiltily at the phone. "You're right: I did take the phone off the hook last night." She couldn't keep her gaze from wandering to Raphael. "I had a lot to think about, and I didn't want to be disturbed."

Margie glanced at Raphael, then back at Gaby. "Hmmmmm, I don't blame you a bit. I wouldn't have wanted to be disturbed either." Margie chuckled knowingly.

"Will you stop with the *hmmmm*'s and tell me

why you're here," Gaby demanded, wishing her secretary didn't have such an active romantic imagination.

Responding to the irritation in Gaby's voice, Margie switched into a more businesslike mode. "There is an important change in today's fashion show. You'll have to rewrite your commentary, so I came over to help you."

"Damn," Gaby muttered under her breath. "I hate last-minute changes. I plan and I plan, and something always happens to mess things up."

Raphael laughed. "Gabrielle, loosen up. You always overplan, then get upset when something overturns your timetable. Have you forgotten my lecture about being a slave to a clock or a schedule? Remember being late to Niko's party? That wasn't so bad, was it?"

As the heat of that memory seared its way into the very core of her being, she did remember. In the dark alone, she wished every night she didn't . . . but she did. Seeking to escape the tormenting desires, she forced her mind to stay strictly on business. Turning her back on him, she asked, "What's the change, Margie?"

"After you left I was straightening up a few last details in the office last night, when this man in a sport jacket you just had to see to believe came barging in, barking orders and generally making himself obnoxious."

Gaby and Raphael exchanged a look. As one they said "Fabian!"

Margie nodded. "That's him. Who is he, anyway?"

"Yes, Raphael, I've been meaning to ask you the same question. I'm curious about a man who sets you up with three dates for dinner."

Raphael frowned. "Fabian's the only thing I don't like about this deal. He works for the PR firm Jean-Claude hired to publicize the line, and he's already a real pain. Like last night: He didn't even ask if I had plans before dragging over those three models he'd found. I want you to understand, when he said everything's arranged the way *we* want it, he meant his PR firm. I had nothing to do with it." He held out his hand toward Gaby. "Am I forgiven, Gabrielle?"

"Oooooh, what chemistry!" Margie sighed. "When you two look at each other, sparks really start to fly. Say, are you the one who sent Gabrielle all the flowers?"

"Yes," Raphael admitted. "I wanted her surrounded by beauty when I returned."

"What a romantic gesture!" Margie sighed again. "You don't happen to have a brother, do you? If so, tell him I'm available, okay?"

"Margie," Gaby said, firmly steering the conversation into safer channels, "if I'm going to rewrite all the commentary, I need to know why. Could we please get back to business?"

"Fabian was talking awfully fast, but I think I got everything straight. Jean-Claude has rushed a set of samples over from Paris and he wants Raphael featured in the show today. That way the new line will be kicked off this season instead of next, as he'd originally planned. He sent three outfits. Oh, and Fabian said Jean-Claude knows this is rushing both of you but to please do it out of friendship." Margie smiled. "There, I think that's all. I've got the clothes out in the car, if you need to see them."

"Did you know about this, Raphael?" Gaby asked.

"No; Jean-Claude promised I would have at least two months to get my affairs—" He paused as his glance flickered with special meaning over Gaby.

"—my *personal* affairs, settled before I got heavily involved in the promotion of the line. I wonder what made him change his mind."

"Don't you know?" Margie gushed. "Haven't you heard the big news? It's so exciting!"

"Slow down, Margie," Gaby urged. "What exciting news are you talking about? Is it something to do with Raphael?"

"You'd better believe it!" Margie turned to Raphael. "Didn't Fabian tell you that that issue of the magazine with your pictures in it sold out in less than a week and *you* were the reason? They practically had a riot in Boston when five women started fighting over the last two copies at a newsstand. They told all about it on the six-o'clock news last night. Didn't either of you see it?"

Gaby shook her head. "I guess we were both busy."

"I'll bet you were!" Margie's brown curls bobbed as she nodded her head knowingly.

Gaby ignored her as she commented, "I suppose the reaction to your magazine layout speeded up Jean-Claude's timetable."

"That's what Fabian said. He said he wanted to promote Raphael while he's a hot property, and that anyone who could set off a riot with just his picture is as hot as they come. He said Raphael's PR potential was dyn-*o*-mite of megaproportions!" She looked at him and sighed. "I agree!"

"Margie, I think you'd better stay away from Fabian. You're starting to sound like a PR person."

"Well," Margie argued, "if he wasn't dyn-a-mite like Fabian said, why would all three television networks be at the Apparel Mart this afternoon to cover the show?"

Gaby's eyes widened in surprise. "They've never done that before."

"They've never had Raphael Salvaje, Raphael the Savage, out promoting a line before," Margie insisted. "I told you, Tom Selleck might as well retire. American women have found a new sex symbol."

Raphael looked decidedly uncomfortable at her description. "That's not exactly what I had in mind when I agreed to get involved in all this," he muttered, running a hand through his black hair. "I think things are getting out of hand. All I wanted to do was find you again, and now . . ."

He let the words fade. The silence stretched as Margie glanced from her boss to Raphael and back again. Finally she insisted, "I'll meet you at the office. You've obviously got better things to do than listen to me run off at the mouth. I've got the clothes, so I'll start on the rewriting of your commentary. Okay?"

Gaby and Raphael, their gazes entwined, were lost in each other and didn't even hear her.

"Never mind. I'll let myself out," Margie muttered, heading for the door. Her hand touched the knob. As she turned it she sighed. "I sure wish I could get someone to look at *me* like that."

CHAPTER FIVE

Suddenly Margie remembered something. She raised her voice to get their attention. "Oh, by the way, Gabrielle, I called Frank. He's waiting outside for you when you're ready."

When the door closed, Raphael raised an eyebrow. "Frank? Who's Frank?"

As the silence stretched, becoming tauter by the second, Gaby could see his frown grow. This time the question was sharper. "Gabrielle, I insist you tell me. Who's Frank?"

He paused, waiting. She lowered her eyes. She couldn't look at him, couldn't admit the irrational fears that turned each ride she took into a nightmare.

In two strides Raphael reached her side. His fingers, curling powerfully over shoulders, demanded an answer. "Who's Frank?" he repeated for the third time. His voice hardened to a new edge. "You accused me of dining with my harem. Maybe you shouldn't have spoken. Is Frank your lover? Gabrielle, tell me! Tell me the truth!"

Finally she forced her gaze up to meet the jealousy blazing in his. The words were choked but she forced them out. "Frank isn't my lover. He's fifty and balding."

81

"That still doesn't answer my question, Gabrielle. Who's Frank and why is he waiting for you?"

Unable to bear looking at him as she admitted the truth, Gaby closed her eyes. "Frank is my chauffeur."

"Your chauffeur?" Raphael's laugh bounced off the walls as his grip loosened. "No wonder you didn't want to tell me. A chauffeur!" he repeated. "And you always throw *my* expensive life-style in my face. You shouldn't talk!"

"You don't understand," she whispered unhappily. "It's not what you think."

"Of course not!" He laughed again. "A chauffeur's not an extravagance. It's just that washing the car might ruin your manicure. Right?"

Strong fingers tilted her face up. "Ah, Gabrielle, don't look so sad. I'll stop teasing you. I just couldn't resist after all the times you've scolded me about my extravagances. Anyway, today you can give him the day off. I've got my car right outside so I can drive you—"

"No!" Gaby choked. "I can't! I . . . I just can't."

"Gabrielle, what is it? Tell me, please. Your eyes are as round and frightened as a child's when she's just coming out of a haunted house."

She pulled from his grasp and moved away so he wouldn't see the tears turning her blue eyes into a sea of pain. "Raphael, it isn't your fault. Believe me, it isn't. It's my problem."

He came up behind her and wrapped comforting arms about her waist. As he laid his face against the softness of her hair he insisted, "If you have a problem, then I have a problem. Tell me, my Gabrielle. Remember, for this one time I am here only to be your friend."

Gaby's hands clenched. "I'm frightened of getting in a car." Once the words started, they tumbled over each other as it all came out. "The nightmares, the terror—I still dream about the accident. Sometimes I wake up shaking. I tried to drive and just froze. I couldn't . . . I couldn't make myself do it. The chauffeur, a big car—they're the only things that have helped."

His embrace tightened painfully around her. *"Dios mío!* What have I done to you? Gabrielle, maybe I should go away. I've done enough to hurt you."

Gaby, hearing the raw agony roughening his voice, twisted around in his arms. She gently took his face between her hands. "Raphael, don't talk like that. It hurts me. None of this is your fault. It's my problem and I'll work it out."

The strain didn't ease from his face. "Can you ever forgive me, Gabrielle?"

A tiny smile trembled on her lips. "Forgive you? No, I can't do that, because I've never blamed you. Don't you know that?"

Raphael gazed down at her for a long moment, trying to find assurance in her eyes for what her lips had said. Finally believing, the hurt vanished, to be replaced by a longing so intense, it robbed her of all defenses when he bent his head toward hers.

At first the touch of his lips was soft, questioning, again seeking assurance that her words had not lied. Then, growing hungry when she didn't pull away, the kiss began to spin its sensual web around them, isolating them from the world, making their silken trap a place neither wanted to escape from.

Lips warm and firm against hers, the unique scent, part spice, part woodsy, belonging only to him; the welcome thrust of his tongue, begging entry to the secrets within her—it was all so tantalizingly familiar that for long moments Gaby relaxed in his arms, reveling in the memories that were now reality again. Her arms wound around his neck, urging a rougher taking, a taking he was only too glad to deliver. Raphael's strong embrace curved her back until her body pressed against the length of his. Through the sheer silk of her negligee she could feel his throbbing need, echoing the arousal building inside her with each stroke of his tongue, each caress of his hand.

At that moment nothing else mattered, not the past, not the present, not the cloudy future. The only thing she needed to live was the feel of his muscles rippling under her exploring hands. The kiss deepened as the tastes of two becoming one enthralled every nerve within her. Their tongues touched, dueled, loved. She almost groaned when Raphael began to draw away from her. Teasing her, he enticed her to follow his retreat until she found remembered sensations as she touched again his lips, his teeth, then the warm well inside his mouth, with strokes of her tongue. No memories of the past intruded to mar the sensual rediscovery of the magic that was special to them.

Gaby felt his hands slip from her back to find the knot holding her robe closed. She knew she should draw away, tell him no, ask him to leave. Instead her fingers, with a will of their own, wove through his hair, forcing his mouth to continue its delicious plundering. A draft swept over her body, for an instant cooling her heated flesh, as the robe fell to the floor. Then his hand found her, and the heat blazed anew, hotter than ever, searing her wherever he touched her.

Her silk nightgown, tied with tiny bows at the shoulder, was the only barrier she had left when

84

Raphael finally drew away from the enticement of her mouth. Her head fell back, giving him the access he demanded as his kisses trailed a path of ownership down the pulse beating wildly in her throat, into the warm valley between her breasts, then back up until his teeth closed over the silky strap. With a tug, one bow came loose.

A satisfied smile played over his lips as he gazed at his handiwork. Then, with a muttered oath and more will power than he knew he possessed, he pushed her a step away from him. Surprised, Gaby's eyes flew open to watch him fight to control his breathing.

"Gabrielle, I'm sorry. I didn't mean to do that. I swore to myself I wouldn't." The rasp in his voice told her what a sacrifice he'd made. "Then, with the tiniest touch, you destroy all my self-control. I want to lose myself in you. I've *never* wanted another woman like I want you."

Struggling for some protection from the overwhelming desire tempting her to forget everything, but feeling the urge to take his hand and lead him into her bedroom, she protested, "I find that a little hard to believe. What with your picture splashed all over the magazines, first with that German beer heiress, then the long, lanky Swedish blonde who was with you in—"

He silenced the words with a kiss, a kiss he didn't allow to deepen to anything more. After he lifted his head he murmured, "Are you trying to pick a fight with me, Gabrielle, by tossing my somewhat rakish past in my face? Well, if you are, it won't work. We are made for love, not bickering. It's our destiny."

Remembering the night of Niko's party, she

countered, "I thought your destiny was to remain free and unfettered."

"Holding you again makes freedom lose some of its appeal—unless, of course, you're talking about the freedom of your bed."

"No, I wasn't."

"I was afraid of that," Raphael admitted ruefully.

She had to make him understand. "Raphael, to be happy I need commitment, a promise for the future; yet, for you to be happy you need freedom. I need security; yet, you'd rather have a Ferrari. Don't you understand why it won't work?"

He winced slightly at her words, and a sadness lurked in his dark eyes as he admitted, "And those are things I can't give you right now."

"I know."

"Gabrielle, don't look at me like that, please. All I'm asking is for you to be patient."

Be patient! That was the story of our whole relationship!

When she remained silent, he tried to bring back her smile by observing, "Well, you have to admit one thing: As we proved a few minutes ago, at least one part of our relationship seems to be working out just great. Or do you deny that? Do you deny that if I hadn't stopped, we probably would have ended up in your bed?"

"Raphael I . . ." Her words faded. How could she deny something her heart knew to be true, even if her mind didn't want to admit it?

"Gabrielle, I won't promise I'll always be this strong, because I won't. Besides, it's your own fault that you're giving me ideas. You shouldn't have thrown yourself at me. How can you expect me not to catch you, catch you and hold you very tight against me?"

"Raphael, I didn't! You were the one who—"

"Gabrielle, calm down." He laughed. "I was only teasing." His eyes grew serious again. "Neither of us can help it that when we touch, fireworks explode all around us. It's been that way from the first day we met. Remember?"

Gaby swallowed, remembering vividly the night of Frederika's party, the silence of the gazebo in the garden where he'd first taken her in his arms, where they first kissed, where they first . . . Damn those memories! They made her almost as weak with longing as his kisses.

She shrugged her shoulders, trying to appear casual. "It must be old age creeping up on me. I can't seem to remember anything special about the evening we met."

Raphael laughed again. "Gabrielle, I keep telling you, you can't lie to me. The truth is in your eyes, the sudden flush to your cheeks. You remember that night as well as I."

The phone rang. With a silent sigh of thanks for the rescue, Gaby grabbed for it. Margie's excited voice blasted through the receiver. "That Fabian fellow is here again. This time he's got photographers from four magazines in tow, and he's demanding to know where Raphael is." She lowered her voice to a whisper. "Do I know where Raphael is?"

Gaby didn't have any trouble understanding her secretary's message. Margie was prepared to lie if they wanted more time alone together. "Tell Fabian his superstar is having breakfast and we'll meet both of you at the Apparel Mart in about an hour. Oh, by the way, how do Jean-Claude's designs look?"

Margie let out a low whistle. "Let's just say when

87

Raphael is introduced this afternoon, he'll be lucky if the female buyers don't mob him. For that matter, some of the men might want a shot too. You know how it is in the big bad world of high fashion." She giggled. "Maybe Fabian should hire some guards to keep the crowd from ripping his clothes off."

"Margie, your imagination is not to be believed!" Gaby chuckled. "But I'll give Raphael your warning."

After she hung up the phone, Raphael asked, "What's the warning?"

"Margie thinks Jean-Claude's designs are, if I may borrow a phrase, so dyn-a-mite, you'll drive the buyers crazy."

Raphael looked dubious. "Is that likely? I'm not a rock star or anything like that."

"Don't worry, Margie gets carried away." Gaby patted his shoulder as she started for the kitchen. "Most buyers have seen it all. It makes them a pretty blasé crowd."

"On the other hand, *you*'ve seen it all, and you weren't so blasé a little while ago," Raphael challenged, following her.

She chose to ignore the shaft of warmth stabbing through her at his words. Instead she asked, "How do you want your eggs? Do you still like them scrambled?"

He leaned against the counter and smiled at her. "Yes, I do. Remember how you'd scramble the eggs, then bring them back to bed so we could eat and—"

"Raphael!" she warned, brandishing a frying pan at him.

"Okay!" He laughed. "I'm hungry, so I'll be good . . . for now."

After they'd eaten and she'd gotten dressed, they

started outside. He was silent as he stared at the big silver Mercedes parked at the curb. His hand clenched. Finally, with a regretful glance at the flashy red Ferrari sitting just behind it, he said, "Gabrielle, I understand why you can't ride with me, so I'll just ask: Does your Mercedes have room for another passenger?"

"Of course," Gaby replied, secretly pleased he chose to ride with her instead of whizzing down the highway in his sports car.

Raphael helped her into the car. Gaby was looking down, so she didn't see him blanch under his tan as she securely buckled her seatbelt in place.

After introducing Raphael to Frank, she ordered, "To the Apparel Mart, please. I suppose you'd better take the Tollway. We need to get there in a hurry." She lowered her voice. "There's a horde of photographers waiting for America's newest hunk."

Raphael wrinkled his nose in distaste. "'Hunk'? You Americans and your slang. I don't think I like the sound of that. It makes me sound like a side of beef."

Gaby ran her hands teasingly up his chest. "Yeah, but what a side of beef!"

Raphael quickly stripped open the buttons on his shirt. "Sounds like you're hungry. You're welcome to take a nibble on this side of beef anytime you want."

For a long fascinated moment Gaby could not draw her gaze away from the rapid rising and falling of his broad chest, a chest that haunted her dreams. The thick mat of black hair, the contours of the muscles, even the very texture of his flesh—she remembered it all. Her fingers itched to reach, to touch, to experience anew. But she fought the temptation by starting to rebutton his shirt.

She forced her voice to stay cool as she observed, slipping the last button through its hole, "There, that's better. Fabian would never forgive us if we got his star hunk busted for indecent exposure."

A knowing smile touched Raphael's lips. "Is it Fabian you're worried about, or yourself, *pollo pequeño?*"

"I am not a chicken!" Gaby retorted, wishing yet again that he didn't know her so well. "I am merely being discreet."

Raphael glanced around at the car, then lowered his voice so only she could hear. "My Gabrielle, you didn't plan very well. While you were getting a big car to protect you from the wild Texas drivers out there, why didn't you get a Cadillac limousine with smoked windows and a glass between your trusty chauffeur and us? Then I could make love to you right now and no one would know."

"I'd know." Her voice came out husky at the thought.

He smiled a smile that brought a flush of warmth to her face. "Yes, you would, my Gabrielle. But I assure you you wouldn't care. It was so good between us and it will be so good again."

"Raphael, don't. Can't you let the past go?" she asked in a strangled voice.

"No! I can't forget those memories and neither can you. They are with me every minute of every day. They fill my soul at night when you are not beside me. And I know you feel the same way!" he insisted almost fiercely under his breath. "Someday I'm going to enjoy hearing you admit it."

For a long moment they looked at each other. Then Gaby opened her mouth to answer, but Frank's question interrupted her. "If you folks are done whispering back there, I've got a question.

What door do you want to be let out at? With all the traffic, the front door would be—"

Suddenly he slammed on his brakes when the car in front of them slowed to a crawl to let the passengers gawk at one of the towering mirrored office buildings being constructed along the Tollway. "Damn tourists," he muttered, noticing the license plate. "Sorry, ma'am. I'll try to keep it nice and smooth from now on."

"Don't worry about it," Gaby managed to say through clenched teeth.

Raphael glanced down at her fingers, twisted into nervous knots, and covered her hands with his. "Gabrielle, look at me. Talk to me. Don't watch the traffic. Tell me how your modeling agency became so successful so quickly."

She knew he was trying to distract her, and the effort pleased her. As she started talking, some of the tension began seeping out of her body. Five miles later she said, "Okay, it's your turn. What's it like not running around on the soccer field, having all the women ogle your legs?" Then the blue of Gaby's eyes softened with concern. "It was part of your life for so long. Do you miss it, Raphael?"

"Sure, I miss all those women throwing their hotel-room keys at me. Who wouldn't?" he joked, then sobered. "I guess the real answer is yes, I miss parts of it, and parts of it I don't. I miss the friendships I made on the team. I miss the roar of the crowd when I scored a goal. But I do not miss practicing in the broiling Madrid sun!" he insisted as the car pulled up in front of the Apparel Mart. When Frank opened the door a blast of searing air hit them. Raphael smiled as he helped her out of the car. "That makes me feel right at home. Thank goodness for air conditioning!"

Gaby smiled, linking her arm through his, and they began walking. "I fervently agree. It certainly helped the South 'rise' again, as the saying goes."

Raphael glanced at her, obviously unfamiliar with the historical allusion, but before he could ask her about it, something else grabbed his attention. He stopped. As his gaze scanned the expanse of the building, he commented, "I had no idea the Apparel Mart was this huge. Last time I came in the side door."

"Mind if we admire it from the inside? I'm melting."

They walked into the crowded lobby and headed for the Great Hall. Gaby explained, "This building, with its million-and-a-half–plus square feet, has turned Dallas into the third largest fashion market in the country. We're behind New York and LA, but we're closing rapidly in on that number-two spot. That's one of the main reasons I decided to return here: The opportunities are endless."

A gaggle of buyers stopped speaking as they neared. They stared at Raphael. With whispers of "Isn't that him?" and "He could put his shoes under my bed anytime!" following them, they hurried toward the Great Hall.

"This is really beginning to get to me!" Raphael muttered under his breath.

"My friend, it comes with the territory!"

"I know. That doesn't mean I have to like it!" he complained. "But I guess there's nothing I can do about it. I'm stuck with this contract. If only I hadn't—"

The words were snapped off so suddenly, Gaby glanced up at him. The thread of frustration beating in his voice didn't escape her, but she had no idea what had caused it.

"If only you hadn't *what?*" she asked.

"Nothing. Forget it."

"How can I? You sound so frustrated about something. Surely it can't be all the attention you're attracting. I thought all men enjoyed being adored," Gaby teased, trying to ease his scowl.

Raphael stopped walking and looked at her. He didn't smile. "They do, but only by the woman they love. Or at least that's how I feel. The rest of it is meaningless." His hand curled warmly about her arm. "I don't suppose you're in an adoring mood, are you?"

"Well"—she drew the word out provocatively—"I might be if . . . if you bought me a cup of coffee. For some strange reason I didn't get much sleep last night. I could use a pep-up shot of caffeine."

He laughed. "A cup of coffee—you mean that's all it takes to turn you from distant to adoring? And I wasted all that money trying to entice you with Dom Pérignon! Your wish is my command. Fabian and his photographers can wait."

As they made their way through the clutter of the cafeteria he changed the subject. "What am I supposed to do today, anyway? Jean-Claude said he did not want me to model. He wants me to represent the line, whatever that means, but he didn't tell me how. That was one of the things we were supposed to work out over the next two months. Now we've got about two hours."

"Yoo-hoo, you two," Margie greeted when she found them by the coffee urn. "I've got the clothes lined up and the new commentary written, but of course you'll want to read it over. I've even reserved the VIP dressing room for you."

"You're so efficient. I'm impressed," Gaby complimented her. In truth she was somewhat surprised. Maybe Margie would turn out to be a jewel of a secretary after all.

"Let's drink our coffee in your dressing room and go over the script," Gaby suggested. "We also have to check to see if all the clothes fit."

"They'll fit. You know Jean-Claude: He's a perfectionist. Before I left Paris he took at least a hundred measurements of me," Raphael assured her.

"Can I come?" Margie begged. "There's this one outfit I can't wait to see Raphael in! I may have to take a tranquilizer. It is really—"

"Yes, we know," Gaby interrupted with a chuckle. "It's dyn-a-mite!"

When they were settled in the dressing room Gaby went over the commentary while Raphael changed. "This is fine, Margie. In fact, it's excellent. The only change I think we'll need to make is—"

The words ended in a gasp as Raphael walked out from behind the screen. Just looking at him, Gaby felt her pulse quicken. Black leather pants stretched skin-tight over the bulging muscles of his legs. His black silk shirt, slashed to the waist, had full sleeves reminiscent of the most swashbuckling buccaneer. A massive gold chain belt accented and completed the outfit.

When she could get her breath she said, "Margie, alert the paramedics. Our female buyers will never survive this. We'll have them fainting all over the place."

Raphael ignored her secretary. His dark eyes, intensified by the black he wore, bore into Gaby with a meaning that fired her already warm blood. She felt as if they were seeing all the way into her soul and reading the desire lurking there.

"And what about you, Gabrielle? Do I have that effect on you?"

"Oh, brother, here they go again," muttered Margie, gathering up the papers. "You obviously don't need me. I'll see you two later, after I locate Fabian and the photographers."

She had just reached the door when there was a loud rap and Fabian barged in. Gaby blinked as the mood shattered. That special moment when she had looked at Raphael and the world disappeared had seemed so unreal. Returning to reality felt like surfacing from deep beneath the sea.

I've got to get ahold of myself! she silently ordered herself. *He walks out in black leather pants and I get light-headed!*

She deliberately turned away to look at Fabian, then wished she hadn't. The orange and black houndstooth coat he had on made her eyes hurt.

"Raphael, my man, you look dyn-a-mite!" Fabian slapped him on the back. "Between my genius for promotion and your brawn, we can't miss! We're going to set this town on its ear. Hell, we're going to set this country on its ear! I'm going to make you the most famous jock in history."

Raphael's grimace was his only answer. Fabian didn't even notice his displeasure. "I've been priming the ol' pump for you. Just wait till you walk out on that runway. You're going to blow those female buyers away." He rubbed his hands together. "It's gonna look great on the news."

Gaby was afraid to ask what Fabian had done to promote the show, and from the look of disgust on Raphael's face, it was obvious he wasn't going to ask either. She just hoped it wasn't in terrible taste. Then she looked at Fabian's jacket again and said a prayer. That was their only hope.

"Raphael, you've got those photographers to meet, and I have to go and check to see if all the models have arrived." She frowned, remembering disasters of the past when some hadn't shown up, leaving her shorthanded. "Punctuality and reliability are not virtues most of them cultivate. It's probably because they're starving to death."

"Wait a minute. We haven't discussed what I'm supposed to do."

"Just stand there. That would be enough for me," sighed Margie.

Gaby frowned a warning at her, then turned back to Raphael. "I'll introduce you, describe what you have on. Then you say a few words about Jean-Claude and his wonderful designs. That's all. I don't think you need to parade up and down the runway."

"No, he'd better not do that," Fabian agreed. "The way I've got this thing set up, he'd get mobbed. 'Course, that would make a great television shot. Maybe you should—"

"No, Raphael you shouldn't," Gaby interrupted firmly. "You are representing the line; you are not a model."

"I agree!" Raphael was visibly relieved. Then he winked at her. "I owe you one. You can collect tonight. And, Fabian, don't you come up with any of your cork-brained ideas. I'm tied up tonight. Understand?"

Fabian nodded, responding to the no-nonsense tone of his voice. "Sure, sure, whatever you say. Now, strike a virile stance. I'm going to let the photographers in."

"That's my cue to leave. Come on, Margie. I'll see you in about an hour, Raphael. Don't worry, you're going to be great."

An hour later Gaby peeked through the curtain at the swirling mob of buyers filling the Great Hall.

Every table was full, they were lined up all around the room, and more were hanging over the balconies that lined the six floors surrounding the open hall. As promised, the three major networks had television crews stationed at the end of the runway. Even away from the floor she could feel the breathless excitement radiating from the expectant buyers.

She turned to Margie. "I've never seen a crowd like this turn out for a fashion show. It's enormous!"

"That's because Dallas has never seen an event like this. 'Raphael the Savage Takes Big D'—I can see the headlines now!"

Gaby shook her head. Yes, she definitely had to keep her secretary away from Fabian. His witless enthusiasm was obviously catching.

Finally she took a deep breath and pushed her way through the curtain. A huge roar of applause, mixed with shouts of "Where's Raphael? We want Raphael!" greeted her entrance.

When the din settled down, she stepped to the microphone. "Gabrielle Presents welcomes you to the fall market couture show." Behind her the low rumble of jungle drums started. "Today we start with the most exciting new look of the year. Hot, primitive, with the thrill of the wild, our first model has on a design by that famous Italian designer Marcantonio. Notice how . . ."

As the commentary rolled on, Gaby felt the usual butterflies settle down and stop fluttering about in her stomach. Each model was greeted with polite applause, but she could sense the air of expectancy grow and spread through the crowd as they waited for Raphael's entrance.

The jungle drums faded, ending the first scene. As the sound of bagpipes began playing softly in the background she continued, "The return to natural fibers continues strong this season. And what is more natural than wool? All the designers are using it, but none so successfully as Jean-Claude in his new men's line. To introduce the line to Dallas and the world, here is Raphael Salvaje."

Before she had even gotten his name out, her voice was drowned out by excited screams from the audience. Raphael seemed a little uncertain as he walked out onstage to the thunderous welcome. The applause, the shouts, the squeals, continued so long and were so loud, Gaby's ears started ringing. She'd never seen any fashion audience so wildly excited before. It sounded like a bunch of teenagers going crazy over the newest rock sensation. The whirl of the cameras caught it all.

With a smile and a wave of his hand, Raphael finally managed to quiet the mob. His speech, touched by his soft Spanish accent, brought sighs and more squeals. Gaby doubted if most of the buyers cared what he said, just as long as he kept standing there, speaking. Finally he escaped and the show went on.

The crowd reaction to his second appearance echoed the wild enthusiasm of the first. He was dressed in a yachting outfit for those winter trips to the Caribbean, and the audience would hardly let him leave the stage. Only when Gaby promised he'd be back in something even more spectacular did the buyers settle down.

His last appearance closed the show . . . in more ways than one. The instant the curtain parted and the buyers saw him in the black leather, they went crazy. The noise was staggering. Whistles, claps, hoots, the thunder of stomping feet, and repeated shouts of "Take it off, take it off!" bounced off the walls. Raphael smiled, but Gaby, knowing him as well as she did, realized under the smile burned a raging anger. She wouldn't have wanted to be Fabian.

Quickly she thanked the audience and said goodbye, then linked her arm through Raphael's and hurried through the curtain backstage. "Where is he?" Raphael growled. "When I get my hands on him, I'm going to kill him."

"Raphael, calm down," she said, trying to soothe his seething temper. Unfortunately for Fabian, it didn't work.

Impervious as usual to the currents flowing around him, the PR man rushed up. "Didn't I tell you it was going to be great! Did you hear the applause, those shouts? This is really going to—"

Raphael's hand curled into a fist. "Fabian, explain! Explain now!"

"Explain what?" Fabian asked with a wide-eyed innocence that wouldn't have fooled a two-year-old.

Gaby moved between the two men. "All right, Fabian, I don't think this is the time for any of your games. Have you been entertaining the buyers at strip joints?"

"Strip joints?" Raphael frowned. "I don't—"

"Yeah, the new kind," Gaby explained. "Where the *men* take off their clothes."

"Fabian, where do you want the remains sent? Because when I get my hands on you, you don't want to know what's going to happen."

Raphael's words and his efficient-looking fist sent Fabian scurrying behind Margie for protection. "You wouldn't hit a guy with a mortgage, would you?" he whined. "Besides, look at the publicity that stunt generated. I may make the PR hall of fame with this one."

"If you live that long!"

"Raphael, my friend, how can you say that?" Fabian protested, staying behind Margie as Raphael advanced. "I've made you a national symbol. You'll be famous."

"I don't want to be famous!"

"Now, now," Fabian said soothingly, still holding Margie in front of him. "It wouldn't look good if you decked your PR agent."

"I won't have a PR agent once I get Jean-Claude on the phone," Raphael warned. "I don't like being hyped like one of your male strippers."

"Remember, we've got a contract. You can't—"

Suddenly someone caught Fabian's eye, and he turned to greet the elderly woman who was eagerly approaching. "Miss Brewster, how are you? And how's business at your Brewster Place stores? How many do you own now, twelve or fifteen? You must come meet, Raphael," he suggested, obviously delighted with the distraction. Under his breath he muttered, "Be nice. She's important."

"We're not finished with this discussion," Raphael informed him in a harsh whisper as he turned to meet the approaching buyer.

"Raphael, you were wonderful," the buyer cooed up at him. Then, almost as an afterthought, she added, "And I loved Jean-Claude's designs. They will be perfect for my chain of stores." She put her hand on Raphael's arm. "Let's talk about it . . . at dinner. I'm staying at the Anatole."

Taking his clue from Fabian, Raphael smiled down at her. "I have shopped in your store in New York and it is fabulous. You're right, Jean-Claude's new line will be perfect for your discriminating customers. However, as much as I would like to dine with you and discuss the line, tonight is impossible. I have an appointment I just can not miss."

Her wrinkles sank into a pout. "Oh, that *is* disappointing." Then she brightened as she coquettishly patted her improbably blue hair. "Maybe tomorrow? Oh, drat, I forgot, I've got to fly to Paris tomorrow to shop Yves Saint Laurent's new collection."

She waited hopefully, but Raphael disappointed her as he nodded. "And I know how important that trip is. I wouldn't think of asking you to delay your flight. Dinner will have to be another time."

Reluctantly, Miss Brewster let go of his arm. "I will see you the next time I am in Dallas." With that ominous promise she turned and walked off.

"I'm afraid you're not out of the woods yet," Gaby whispered as she identified the group of hovering buyers who were eyeing him with great interest. "Neiman-Marcus, Bloomingdale's, Lord & Taylor, Marshall Field, and Saks. Looks like you've hit the big time."

"No I haven't. There is nothing in my contract with your friend, Jean-Claude, that says I have to take being mauled by a group of blue-haired old hens." He grabbed Gaby's arm. "We're getting out of here."

"I can't. I've got to get all the clothes back to the showrooms."

"Let Margie do it. Fabian can help her." Raphael snapped his fingers as he nervously watched the approaching herd of buyers. "No, I've got a better idea." He raised his voice to get Fabian's attention. "Fabian, I'll let you off the hook this time if you'll intercept that advancing horde. Use your expense account. Wine and dine them, take them to the theater—I don't care. Just no more strip joints! Understand!"

Fabian shrugged. "Sure, sure, keep your pants on."

As they turned away, Raphael chuckled to himself. "That's the one thing I have no intention of doing!"

CHAPTER SIX

With an arm firmly around Gaby's waist, Raphael guided her out of the Apparel Mart. The sun was setting, but the hot humid air still smothered them like a heavy wool blanket. While they waited for Fred to weave his way through the heavy traffic to reach them, Gaby teased, "Come on, tell me the truth. I know you were mad at Fabian, but didn't part of you love it when all those women yelled, 'Take it off, take it off'? That must have made your ego grow to Texas-size proportions."

Unconsciously his shoulders straightened. "Well, it was sort of a thrill. But I'd enjoyed that feeling a lot more if you were the one yelling, 'Take it off.' I'd be out of these clothes so fast, you wouldn't have time to run. Shall we try it and see how it works?"

"In front of all these people? How brazen you Spaniards are!"

His eyes blazed as he looked down at her. No smile softened his determination. "Yes, we are. We're brazen enough to win *any* woman. You'd better accept that. You can fight but *I* will win. I will have you in my bed again . . . and soon. There is no other woman for me. There is no other man for you. That's our fate."

"Raphael I . . ." The words faded, as Gaby couldn't meet the fierce possession in his gaze.

As she looked down at the concrete she shivered. He was as certain as she was uncertain. She wanted him—she knew that with every breath she took. She wanted his kisses to blot out her doubts. She wanted his caresses to ignite a fire so hot, only having him inside her again could put it out. The desire raged; yet, in her heart she knew having him in her bed would only satisfy part of her need.

What about her needs for the future? In Europe he'd been wild, irresponsible, always taking risks, refusing to settle down. Had anything changed? Look at his life-style: a penthouse, a Ferrari . . . He was as extravagant as ever.

Another thing worried her too: She'd been the only woman ever to tell him good-bye. How could she be sure it wasn't only his Spanish pride that demanded her surrender? Once he'd conquered her, would the challenge be over and his interest wane? Losing him a second time might be a break she'd never recover from. No plaster cast can mend a broken heart. Wasn't it safer just to let things stay the way they were? But if she did that . . .

"Gabrielle, is anything wrong?" Raphael asked, touching her arm. "You're muttering 'Damn, damn, damn' under your breath."

A guilty flush reddened her cheeks. She hadn't even been aware she'd spoken. Luckily, before she had to reply, Frank arrived with the Mercedes.

Once the car rolled away, Raphael asked, "You were quiet so long back there. Does that mean you've finally accepted what will be?"

"No." She smiled, deliberately shoving all the doubts far back in her mind. She enjoyed being with Raphael. Why tangle up her feelings with a bunch of questions that had no answers? "Actually, I enjoy a challenge just as much as you do. The silence simply meant I was thinking up a clever way to thwart fate."

"It can't be done."

In a secret place in her heart she feared he was right, but that didn't mean she wasn't going to fight.

"Well, I know one thing: Thwarting fate can't be done on an empty stomach."

Raphael laughed. "Is that a not-too-subtle way of saying you want me to take you out to dinner?"

"Well, after all, why should I cook when you've got an unlimited expense account?" Gaby pointed out logically. "And as you told me the night you dined with your harem, part of your job is to be out and about on the town so all the women can ogle you and all the men will rush out and buy Jean-Claude's designs, hoping some of those ogles will get tossed in their direction."

"Okay, you win. Where shall I get ogled tonight? The Mansion, Agnew's, La Louvre? You pick a restaurant."

Gaby twisted in her seat to face him. "Do you know what I really want tonight?"

"Well, I sure know what *I* want! And it has nothing to do with food!"

"Raphael, quit changing the subject. You said I could pick the restaurant."

"Okay, what's it going to be? We can get to what I want later."

Gaby ignored his quip as she licked her lips in anticipation. "I've got the wildest craving for fried clams. How about going to Howard Johnson's."

"Howard Johnson's? You're kidding."

"No, Raphael, I'm not. I love their clams and I haven't had any in ages."

Raphael shook his head in disbelief. "I offer to lay the world of haute cuisine at your feet, and all you want is fried clams. Okay, Frank, take us to Howard Johnson's."

The chauffeur glanced over his shoulder. "Ma'am, you know we'll have to use North Central to get there."

Gaby swallowed a tremor of fear at having to travel on the narrow, congested expressway. "For fried clams I can brave even Central Expressway."

As the car picked up speed Raphael curled his arm around her shoulders and drew her protectively against him. "Feel safer now?"

"From the traffic, yes. From you, no."

His satisfied chuckle filled the car. "Ah, that means we're making progress." He lowered his voice so only she could hear. "You know, I'm beginning to like this chauffeur idea. He can drive and we can neck."

"Raphael!"

"What, no neck?" He chuckled. "That's okay, I'm easy to please. I'll settle for ear." He leaned over and whispered, "You have a wild craving for clams. Any other wild cravings I should know about? I'm willing to satisfy *every* desire you have."

The words, blown softly in her ear, sent a curl of longing spiraling through her body. Raphael knew her so well. He knew just where to touch her to stir her blood. He knew every secret spot that seduced her willpower until she was so weak with wanting, she'd do anything.

"You're not playing fair. You know what blowing in my ear does to me."

"Of course I do, my Gabrielle. That's why I'm doing it. I remember every erotically sensitive part on your delightful body and plan to arouse them all if that's what it takes. I want you too much to play fair. I will use *any* tactic to bring you back to me."

The words faded as his tongue darted out, licking a trail of fire around the delicate shell of her ear, then sending stabs of heat through her as he thrust it into the sensitive interior.

"Raphael, please," she moaned softly, fighting the delicious weakness tempting her to forget the fried clams and order Frank to head for her house so she and Raphael could trade the backseat of her car for the privacy of her bedroom.

"Please what, my love?" he whispered, blowing softly with each word. "Please make love to you? That's what I want more than anything in this world. Tell me it's what you want too."

His warm breath, husky with a longing she was so dangerously familiar with, blew its own message into her ear, a message her body responded to instinctively.

"But . . . ooooh, Raphael," she sighed as sensations too delicious to ignore began penetrating every part of her. They smothered every instinct but the one driving her toward Raphael and all the pleasure only he could give. No! Don't! Her mind tried to scream. But sensation totally muffled the warning with a plea of its own to give him exactly what he wanted and what her own body craved.

"Answer me, my Gabrielle. Tell me your blood isn't hot with wanting me. Tell me you don't feel right now the same incredible kind of excitement we shared three years ago."

She tried to pull her head away, but strong hands captured her as the sweet torment went on. "Yes, I remember what blowing in your ear does to you. You become wild. You become an insatiable lover."

Her eyes closed as the breath blowing in her ear drove everything away, leaving only blazing need. Her body felt on fire as he stopped speaking and began teasing her again with moist strokes of his tongue. His hand found her breast. Aching with a need of its own, it seemed to swell outward to meet him.

Then the inflaming words began again, seducing her, enthralling every nerve, until her whole body throbbed, begging for relief—a relief only having him full and hard inside of her could satisfy. "Tell me, my Gabrielle. Tell me you will be mine again . . . tonight. Let fate win. The loss will be sweet, I promise."

"Hey, folks, we're here," Frank called. "Two plates of fried clams coming up."

"Oh, damn!" Raphael muttered.

Gaby took longer to respond. Frank's words slowly pulled her out of the fog of desire cloaking her mind. So intense were the sensations aroused by Raphael's whispered words that she hadn't even realized they'd stopped in front of the restaurant.

"Well, folks, are you just going to sit there?" Frank demanded, holding open the door. "I thought you were hungry."

"I *am* hungry," Raphael muttered, "but not for clams!"

Gaby didn't honestly know if she was glad that they'd reached the restaurant. She knew only that if Raphael had had a few more minutes, there was no doubt about how she'd have answered his question. Maybe she should thank her craving for fried clams for rescuing her this time . . . but she wasn't sure.

"Come on, we're here," she urged, grabbing his hand. "We might as well eat."

"I guess you're right. It's been a long time since our late breakfast, and you know what they say: no food, no energy." Raphael winked at her. "And I

108

want you full of energy tonight. The moon stays up there a long, long time."

An hour later they walked back outside. Raphael patted his stomach. "Well, that took care of one hunger." Suddenly his eyes blazed. "I just remembered: Howard Johnson's is also a motel. That should make it easy to take care of my other 'hunger.'"

"A tryst in a motel? You're slipping, Raphael. Where's your flair, your originality? I don't think 'sinning' at Howard Johnson's is quite your style."

"Where do you want to 'sin'? You pick the place," he countered.

"Oh, good, here comes Frank," she exclaimed, glad for an excuse to evade his question.

"Saved by your trusty chauffeur once again," Raphael complained. "I'm going to have to have a talk with him. He's interfering with this seduction scene."

After Gaby snapped her seat belt in place, she suggested, "If you promise to behave, I'll invite you in for a nightcap."

"If I behave, neither one of us will have any fun. Lean over here. Let's have some more ear-nibbling."

Her hands came up to hold him off. "No, let's not. You about drove me crazy on the way over here."

Raphael's teeth flashed in a wide grin. "I know, and I'm going to do it again . . . and again . . . and again tonight. But you're right. We'll wait until we get to your place. There's only so far you can go in a car on Central Expressway, even with a chauffeur doing the driving."

"That's not what I—"

Raphael caught a movement out of the corner of his eye. "Gabrielle, watch out," he shouted as an oncoming car, skidding wildly out of control, careened across the grassy lane divider and directly into their path.

Like a kaleidoscope of terror, scenes from their earlier crash, intermixed with the vision of the car sliding at them, shot in terrible confusion through her mind. A scream—one remembered from three years ago or one being wrenched from her throat now? In her terror Gaby really didn't know as the sound echoed through her ears. Again she felt Raphael's arms go around her. Again she tasted fear. So familiar, so horribly familiar. "Not again! Dear God, not again!" she prayed, unaware she'd even spoken.

Gaby watched in fascinated horror as Frank slammed on the brakes and whipped the wheel hard to the left, desperately trying to avoid the oncoming car. A sickening crunch of metal hitting metal jarred them. Then the other car skidded on past, hit the shoulder, and began to roll.

Gaby couldn't stop shaking as Frank managed to get the Mercedes onto the shoulder of the road and stopped. He got out to inspect the damage. Raphael's comforting arms never left her, but even that didn't help her stop the trembling. She closed her eyes, not wanting to see, but the scenes playing in her mind were more terrifying than any reality, so she forced them open again.

After what seemed like an eternity, but in reality was half an hour, Frank climbed back into the car. He twisted around to look at her. "Could have been a whole lot worse, ma'am. The other car only clipped the bumper. Apparently the other guy blew a tire and lost control."

"Any word on the other driver?" Raphael asked. "With the car rolling like that, it looked like—" He stopped speaking when he felt Gaby shudder in his arms.

"That guy'd better get down on his knees every night and thank God for seat belts. He's battered and bruised, but the paramedics said he is going to be all right."

"We've got to get Gabrielle home. Is the car drivable?"

Frank nodded. "Ought to be. As I said, mainly it just messed up the bumper. Ma'am, are you all right? You look mighty pale."

"Just get me home, please," Gaby begged, unable to say any more.

"Take it slow, okay, Frank?" Raphael requested. "Gabrielle's had about all she can take."

The chauffeur nodded in sympathy and started the car. When they started to move, Gaby couldn't stop a shiver from snaking through her. Raphael felt it but didn't say anything as he continued to hold her as close against him as her seat belt would allow. His murmured words of comfort hardly penetrated the haze of her misery.

When they reached her house, he took her hand and didn't let go of it until he poured her a strong shot of calming brandy. "Here, drink this. It will help."

The fiery drink burned down Gaby's throat, a throat raw from her frantic scream. She winced but took another sip. When she set the snifter down on the coffee table, Raphael gathered her up in his arms. For long moments he just held her close, rocking her like a child, trying to ease the terror that still gripped her.

She felt so warm, so secure, in his arms that gradually the trembling slowed and her breathing grew less ragged. In a hesitant voice she whispered, "I feel so foolish. Inside I know it's irrational. I try not to be afraid, and yet I can't help myself. Tonight, when I saw that car sliding at us, I—"

He laid a silencing finger across her lips. "Don't talk about it. Don't think about it. It's over. We're safe. You're in my arms and nothing can hurt you. Remember only good times. Think about the time we were . . ."

Slowly, as his soothing words continued she began to relax. He was so gentle with her, so caring. Finally with a sigh Gaby felt the last tremor leave her body and she lay quietly. Still, she didn't move from the protecting, sheltering warmth of his embrace.

The grandfather clock had just finished chiming eleven when she finally stirred. When she raised her head from Raphael's shoulder and looked at him, her hand went out toward him instinctively. Eyes dull and dark with sadness, a deep frown furrowing his broad forehead, his mouth, usually smiling, now taut and unhappy, she could see his pain carved on every feature.

"Raphael, don't look like that—please don't. I keep telling you, this isn't your fault."

"Gabrielle, no words can ease my guilt about what I've done to you." His fingers twined with hers. "You're still trembling. And I did this to you."

With gentle strokes of her fingers Gaby tried to smooth the frown from his forehead. When that didn't work, she tried to ease the tension with a tiny joke. "Maybe it's your presence that's making me tremble."

His hand curled into an angry fist, an anger directed at himself. "*Dios mío,* how I wish it was, but I know it isn't. Gabrielle how can I help you? There must be something I can do."

112

She shook her head. "There's nothing anyone can do. This is something I have to solve on my own. I have a friend who's a psychologist, and I talked to her about my feelings. She gave my fears a fancy name, something-phobia, and said only time or a miracle will change the way I feel about stepping into a car."

"What do you mean, a miracle? What saint do we pray to?"

Gaby laughed a sad laugh. "I'm afraid it doesn't work that way. The psychologist said sometimes a single event will trigger a recovery, but there's no way of knowing what that might be." She shuddered. "Obviously almost being involved in another serious accident isn't it."

Raphael's fingers tightened about hers. "What will happen if you have this breakthrough?"

"Then I can go on with my life. I'll go back to being a nervous rider, like I was in Europe, instead of being a terrified one."

For the first time he smiled. It wasn't a big smile, but he did smile. "That means you'll go back to slamming your foot through my floorboard and gasping every time I pass a car." He paused and bent to place a kiss on the tip of her nose. "It would be worth it to have you over this phobia thing. I promise I'll never complain."

"Not even when I grab on to the armrest? You once accused me of trying to yank it out of the door."

"I won't complain even when you do that." Something on the coffee table caught his attention. "This is probably the reason we almost had an acci— ah, we had trouble tonight. You forgot to wear your lucky unicorn. Here, let me put it on."

She smiled as she looked at the tiny gold unicorn

dangling on the chain. She'd taken it off the night before and hadn't bothered to put it away. Sweeping her hair up off the nape of her neck, she turned her back to him so he could fasten the necklace. After the clasp was in place, he kissed the area of her skin warmed by the heavy fall of her dark red hair. She half expected him to start nibbling, because he knew the back of her neck was another one of those sensitive zones, but after the one kiss he drew away.

Raphael leaned back against the corner of the sofa, then held out his arms. "Come here, my love."

When she was cuddled snugly against his shoulder, he asked, "When did you take a liking to unicorns? You've got them everywhere—pictures, statues, bookends, necklaces. I don't remember you having them in your apartment in Paris."

"Jean-Claude started me collecting them," Gaby reminisced. "He brought me one in the hospital." She smiled. "He said it was a thing of beauty, of fantasy, a thing not of this world."

"That sounds like you, my Gabrielle."

She laughed. "That's exactly what *he* said. Do you both use the same ghost writer to do the lines you hand out?"

His arms tightened about her. "That's not a line and you know it, my Gabrielle." He was quiet for a long instant. When he spoke again, there was a trace of pain in his voice. "Gabrielle, you let Jean-Claude see you in the hospital but you wouldn't let me. Why? I went through hell, waiting every day on the other side of that door, not knowing if you hated me, not knowing if I'd ever see you again. And then when you started returning my letters unopened, I began to lose hope."

114

"You know why. Our affair was over. There was nothing left to say."

"If it's over, how come you're here, lying in my arms? If it's over, how come this evening on the way to the restaurant I could feel your passion. You wanted me, and nothing you can say will make me believe you didn't."

She twisted around so she could look at him. "Raphael, maybe passion just isn't enough for me anymore. I told you I need commitment. I need roots. I need security. Yes, we could resume our affair, but where would it go? Do we have a future?"

"We can if you believe in it." His eyes were serious. "We can if you'll be patient. I'll work it out somehow."

Gaby sighed unhappily. "That all sounds so vague."

Raphael didn't look any happier. "That's all I can offer you right now. All I know is, we belong together. I knew it in Europe; I'm even more sure now."

"You knew it in Europe?" Gaby asked, one eyebrow raised skeptically. "Was that while you were skiing in Saint Moritz or skin diving in the Aegean?"

Raphael frowned. "You aren't going to let me forget that, are you?"

"Why should I?"

"You should because I wouldn't have been with those other women if it hadn't been your fault."

Gaby's back stiffened. "What? It's *my* fault you went running all over Europe, chasing first one woman and then another?"

"That's right," Raphael insisted firmly. "It's *your* fault. You wouldn't let me see you in the hospital, you returned my letters unopened, then you just dropped out of sight. I tried to find you. I even called your parents, but they—" Suddenly he froze, unable to look at her. "They said I'd hurt you enough and to leave you alone."

"They never told me that."

Raphael shrugged. "I guess I can't blame them after what had happened. Anyway, after all of that, I finally said to hell with it. You'd walked out on me. I didn't need you, I told myself. So I tried to burn you out of my system. Yes, I partied with Niko. Yes, I skied at Saint Moritz. Yes, I held other women, made love to other women. But it didn't help. Instead of forgetting you, my feelings only grew stronger."

Gaby's eyes widened in surprise as Raphael opened his heart to her in a way he'd never done before. "Maybe I became so entranced with the blinding passion of our affair, I didn't realize that under that passion lay a feeling I'd never had for another woman. I don't know. Maybe it took losing you to make me realize what I'd had, what I must have again!" His dark eyes kindled. "Gabrielle, I'll do whatever it takes, wait however long it takes, to make you believe we belong together."

They gazed at each other, not speaking for long moments. Gaby felt so many things, remembered so many things. She remembered the strength of his arms when she trembled. She remembered his gentle caring, his patience as her fears slowly calmed. The words he'd just spoken touched her heart in a way she'd never experienced before. He'd opened his soul to her. Could she do less?

Her hands framed the rugged contours of his face. Her voice sounded whispery-soft; yet, no doubts stopped her as she admitted, "If you asked me tonight to make love to you, I don't think I could say no."

Raphael captured both her hands and brought them to his lips. After kissing each finger, a caring smile touched the corners of his mouth. "Don't you realize, my Gabrielle, that this is the one night I can't ask? You're too vulnerable. I want you. I want you so badly, I ache with that need. But you must come willingly into my arms. It must be your choice. I can't force you into my bed, or take advantage when you're still shaky after what you've been through tonight."

Tears glistened in her eyes when he finished speaking. As one tear trickled down her cheek, he bent to kiss it away. "I didn't mean to make you cry."

A quivering smile shone through her tears. "Sometimes people cry because they're happy."

"Surrounded by happiness—that's how I want to see you." Raphael shoved a cushion behind his back, then snuggled deeper into the corner of the sofa. As he drew her back against him he insisted, "I wanted to spend this night with you in my arms. This isn't exactly what I'd planned, but it has to be."

"I don't understand."

"You didn't think I'd leave you alone tonight, did you?"

"But, Raphael, it isn't necessary for you to—"

He laid one fingertip over her lips, quieting her protest. "Gabrielle, let me do this for you. I wasn't with you to comfort you when that car accident turned your dreams into nightmares. Tonight I want to be here for you in case the nightmares return."

He cuddled her close. "So come, sleep, my love. You'll be safe in my arms."

117

CHAPTER SEVEN

Warm and secure in Raphael's arms, no nightmares disturbed Gaby as she slept. Dawn's light had brightened to a morning blaze when she finally stirred. The roar of the ocean? No, the sound was too regular for that. A clock? No, the sound wasn't quite right. Tiny Infant Heartbeat? Why would her favorite childhood doll be in her living room?

Then finally her sleepy mind put the pieces together and she realized the comforting sound beneath her ear was the steady reassuring thump, thump, thump of Raphael's heart. She smiled as slowly the memories of the night before returned. But instead of remembering the terror of their accident, all that filled her mind were happy thoughts of Raphael and his kindness.

"I thought you were my favorite doll," she mumbled, prying her eyes open, only to close them quickly against the glare of the morning sun streaming in through the double French doors.

"What an opening to start the day! If I'm your favorite doll, then *play* with me," Raphael challenged, wrapping his arms tighter around her.

"It's too early in the morning for games."

"Ah, how familiar. I'd forgotten, you aren't a morning person. It takes two cups of coffee before you're civil."

"I'm not that bad," Gaby protested, twisting around in his embrace so she could argue. "If you remember . . ."

The dark circles shadowing his eyes stopped her words. Concerned, she ran a fingertip over them. "Raphael, did you get any sleep last night? You look awful."

"I make an unbelievable sacrifice to play the noble knight, and you tell me I look awful. Thanks a lot, Gabrielle."

Gaby patted his cheek. "Ah, poor Raphael. How about it if I make amends by feeding you breakfast?"

His black eyes glittered. "How about making amends by trading this sofa for your bed?"

"I'm shocked!" she commented with a laugh. "A noble knight would never make such a scandalous suggestion."

"This noble knight would, especially after the night I spent. Holding you but not being able to really touch you. Having you so close, yet not being able to kiss you. It was hell! Thank God it's morning and I can go back to my normal raffish self."

Gaby reached up and kissed him softly on the mouth. " 'Raffish self'? I think there was a lot of the *true* Raphael in what you did last night. You'll never know what it meant to me. It was one of the most special nights I've ever spent. I'll never forget your kindness, your caring, your patience, your—"

"My stupidity for letting you lie in my arms undisturbed," he interrupted with a laugh. Then his smile faded. "Last night was special for me, too, Gabrielle. Are you sure you're all right now?"

"Yes, sleeping in your arms would calm a hurricane. But I'm worried about you. I think I was taking up most of the space on the sofa. You don't look

119

like you got any sleep," she observed for the second time.

"What man could sleep with you in his arms. I just held you close to my heart, let the hours flow by as I watched you . . . and plotted."

"And plotted?" she asked. "Plotted what? Are you going to take up writing?"

"Hardly!" he laughed. "No, I plotted my strategy of conquest. Last night we called a temporary truce, but today—ah, today, with you being recovered—is another story." He chuckled wickedly. "Today I return to the attack."

"You make me sound like the opposing army. I'm not sure I like— Raphael what are you doing?"

Before she could react, he deftly eased her over until she lay beneath him on the sofa. As his body followed her down Gaby felt a burst of sensation fire through her. The seductive feel of his heavily muscled legs trying to work their way between hers, the remembered weight as he settled his body down upon her, the heat sparking out of his dark eyes as he feasted his gaze on her full moist lips—three years; yet, it remained as fresh a memory as if he'd made love to her yesterday.

Her lips parted in protest, but his kiss snatched the words away. With no barriers to get past this time, his tongue plunged hungrily into the warm intimate interior of her mouth. It was welcome plundering as she returned his kiss with an eagerness that startled her. How could she resist him? Why did she even want to try?

All her doubts, all her questions, dissolved like ice melting in the sun, leaving only desire. Long, tantalizing moments later Raphael finally drew away from the sweetness of her kiss. "Ah, Gabrielle, how right it feels to have you like this again. This is where you belong . . . forever."

She blushed at the intense possessiveness beating through his words. She sighed and admitted, "It does feel good, but staying in this position forever is going to make it a little difficult to do business, isn't it?"

"Gabrielle, your sense of humor is one of the things I love about you, but right now is not the time to crack jokes," he scolded. "We've got more important things to do."

"What things? Cook breakfast? Get dressed? Head for the office?" she teased, winding her arms around his back to let him know she had no intention of doing any one of those things.

"You seem a little dense this morning. Maybe I'd better demonstrate what I have in mind," he murmured, fiddling with the top button of her blouse.

Gaby wiggled beneath him, enjoying the feel of his body pressing her into the softness of the sofa cushions. "Hmmm, that sounds like a good idea. As you pointed out, until I have my coffee, I'm a slow starter."

He winked as the first button on her lacy blouse came loose. "I think I can come up with some way to *stimulate* you and get you moving this morning."

"Will it be better than coffee?" she whispered, already feeling the excited tingles begin to spread through her body.

"You'd better believe it!" Raphael vowed. "Now, shhh, my love. Let me demonstrate. Close your eyes. Dream of how it was between us and how it will be again."

Gaby's eyes closed as she abandoned herself to the man beginning to do such magical things to her body. Button after pearl button slipped through their holes as he worked on the front of her blouse.

When the last escaped, he sighed, "Ah, Gabrielle, still so modest. You insisted on wearing a swimsuit top in Saint-Tropez, and now I find a bra. That's something you never wore in Europe."

His fingertips traced over the lace shielding her secrets from him. As he touched her, her nipples tightened, thrusting against the sheer lace, begging in their own way to be free. When he saw the reaction he laughed. "Covered, but still I know you. Your lips may say, 'Raphael this can't be,' but your body, this gorgeous body, speaks proudly for itself . . . and it does not lie."

Gaby stirred beneath him. Driven to feel more of him, seeking a peace that would end the torment turning her body into one aching throb of need, she arched, inviting a more intimate possession.

"Ah, Gabrielle, you always rush. Let the desire build. The reward will be sweeter," he murmured, slipping a hand under her back to unhook her bra.

She almost moaned when her breasts were finally freed from the brassiere. As she knew he would, he bent to savor the fullness of the breasts she offered. His mouth touched, at first tentatively, almost as if he were waiting for her to tell him to stop. Then, when she stayed silent, his mouth consumed, sucked, licked, drove her almost to the edge of reason. He began to build a fire so hot within her, nothing, not logic or fear or concern for the future, could squelch it.

Blind, with eyes closed, and yet, she saw. Like a movie watched for the dozenth time, she knew how Raphael looked when he bent to kiss her, how he smiled when the last button on her blouse fell free, how the heat of his passion turned his eyes into burning coals when his gaze raked over her naked body. Even without seeing him, she loved the way she knew he looked at her.

Her blouse gone, her bra gone, his kisses began to edge lower across the sensitive bare regions above her skirt. When his hands lifted her hips to reach the zipper to remove that last obstacle, her eyes finally fluttered open and she put her hands out to stop him.

"Gabrielle, no, you can't say no now!"

The admission slipped from her heart. "Maybe I should, but I don't think I could. Raphael, I want to see you as you see me. I'm half naked, yet you're still dressed. Don't you think that's a bit unfair."

His breathing pounded hard, but he managed to smile. "And what do you suggest we do to remedy that 'unfortunate' situation. I am *very* opposed to rebuttoning your blouse, so . . ." He stretched the word out, waiting.

Gaby smiled as she looked into his eyes and found no doubt lurking there. "Sooooo, we make things equal." Her hands reached for the front of his shirt. "I always believe in people being equal."

"Oh, great. Am I going to get a women's-lib lecture now?" Raphael protested. "That idea doesn't go over so great in Spain."

"Shhhh, my fabulous Spaniard," Gaby ordered, unbuttoning the first button of his navy blue silk shirt. "What you're going to get is your own demonstration!"

"But I'm not sleepy," he teased.

"You will be . . . after an hour or two," she promised, unhooking button number three.

As his shirt came open, her hands eagerly reached to touch him, to rediscover the sensations that had driven her to ecstasy three years before in

123

Europe. "Raphael, I love touching you. No man feels as good as you do."

Without warning, his hands snapped down on hers, stopping the motion. "How do you know? How many have you experimented on?"

Gaby looked up, met his unwavering gaze, and spoke the truth. "I only love when I *love* Raphael."

"Gabrielle, I'm sorry," he said softly, gently cupping her breast with one warm hand. "My jealousy flames as hot as my desire."

"It's that hot Spanish blood of yours?" she joked.

"And what's your excuse? You flame hot and you don't have a drop of Spanish blood in those gorgeous veins."

Gaby laughed, happy and free from any doubts for the first time in three years. "It must be osmosis: I caught it from you." The laughter faded, replaced with desire as she whispered, "Raphael love me . . . love me now!"

Willingly she raised her hips to let his hand slide the zipper of her skirt free. Soon only one wisp of silk stood between her and her surrender. It was a surrender made sweeter with the fulfillment of endless dreams.

"Now you," she said, reaching for the front of his slacks, a front not flat and smooth, a front leaving no doubt of his desire. The zipper stuck, then slowly began sliding down. Gaby had almost reached her goal when the pounding started.

"Raphael, open the door." Fabian's jarring voice interrupted the perfect moment. More pounding. "Come on, I know you're in there. We've got work to do—big doings today that can't wait."

"Damn it!" The oath was wrenched from Raphael's soul. "I don't believe it. First Frank and now Fabian. I may go on a rampage and dispose of any man whose name begins with *F*."

"If we ignore him, maybe he'll go away," Gaby whispered.

"Raphael, it's no use," Fabian yelled through the door. "Margie told me where you are. Look, I've made arrangements that just can't wait. Open the door or I'll call someone to kick it in. This is important!"

"I don't think he's going to go away," Raphael said. "I'll tell you what," he snarled in exasperation, "you take care of Margie and I'll deal with Fabian, and then maybe we can have some peace to . . . to enjoy each other." With a frustrated sigh he lifted himself off of her.

With angry jabs Raphael shoved his buttons back in place, zipped his pants, then started for the door. But his steps faltered when he couldn't resist the urge to look back at the woman he'd left on the sofa.

Gaby's soft breasts, still taut with wanting, spilled out of the disheveled lace of her blouse. "Damn it, Gabrielle. Button that blouse, or I swear, Fabian is going to see one hell of a passionate scene when he kicks in the door."

Obediently she resecured her blouse and tucked it demurely into the waistband of her linen skirt. Only then did Raphael reluctantly unlock the door.

"Raphael, my man, do I have news for you," Fabian chortled, barging past him into the room. "Every network in the area wants an interview. I've got photo sessions set up for six different magazines, and wait until you hear the big news!"

His string of "wonderful" announcements was interrupted by the shrill ringing of the telephone. Gaby grabbed the offending instrument and snapped, *"What is it?"*

125

"Hey, you don't need to take my head off," Margie protested.

"Margie, I'm sorry. I didn't mean to snarl at you" —she glanced at Raphael—"but it's been one helluva morning."

"Look, I'm sorry to bother you so early, but we've got a huge problem here. Also, I wanted to warn you that Fabian came raging into the office, demanding to know where—"

"Margie, Fabian's here now. What's the problem at the office?"

"It's about the show for the dental convention. They don't want to hold it in the regular place at Reunion Arena, so we'll have to dress a stage set. I've already called your decorator to bring in some ideas, but I really think you need to be—"

"Yes, I know," Gaby admitted wearily. "I really need to be there. See you soon," she said, efficiently cutting short one of Margie's rambling conversations.

Gaby turned to the two men, still huddled by the door. "Raphael, I have to—"

He spoke at the same time: "Gaby, I have to—"

"Sounds like we both have a full day ahead of us," she admitted sadly.

Quickly he moved to her side and lowered his voice as he pressed the key to his apartment into her hand. "Give me this evening. Come to my penthouse. We'll take the phone off the hook. We'll disconnect the door chimes. We'll tell the security officer not to let anyone up."

"Do you really think we can keep reality from intruding, Raphael?" she pleaded as the demands of her job, the demands of his job, seemed determined to keep them apart.

"Just wait, I'll work something out. Gabrielle, we came so close. You were almost mine."

"I know. Maybe I should thank Fabian for keeping that from happening."

The hurt darkened his eyes. "You don't mean that."

After last night she couldn't lie anymore. "No, Raphael, I don't mean that."

His smile almost blinded her as he swept her up in his arms and whirled her around. "I want to tell the whole world you belong to me," he shouted happily.

"You can't do that!" Fabian quickly intervened.

Raphael stumbled, startled at the other man's interruption. They were both so happy, they'd almost forgotten Fabian was there. After setting her back on her feet, he demanded, "What in the hell do you mean by that? Why can't I?"

"Because I've just signed a contract with *Gentlemen's Quarterly* to have you named one of the ten most eligible bachelors in America. It's going to be a huge feature article, and I've even finagled you the cover shot. It will be a dyn-a-mite way to publicize Jean-Claude's new line. So you're going to have to keep this little lady under wraps until the article is printed. That was one of about a dozen things I need to talk to you about."

Raphael tapped his fingers irritably against his leg, obviously unhappy at Fabian's news. "If I could, I'd take that damned contract and tell Jean-Claude where to put it."

"Well, you can't and you know it," Fabian said reasonably. "We've got a lot of people to see and plans to make, so come on."

Raphael turned to her. "Gabrielle, I'm sorry. Promise me we'll have dinner together tonight."

127

She took a deep breath. "I wish I could promise, but I can't. A big problem's come up about the next fashion show. I'll try to be free, but I don't know." Her hand touched his arm. "Call me when you have time."

"I wish I had time to do a lot more than that!" he muttered.

She squeezed his arm. "Weren't you the one who told me to be patient, that it makes 'everything' sweeter?"

"Tonight seems like a long way off." Raphael sighed, letting his gaze wander lovingly over her face, then down to her lacy front.

"I know," Gaby agreed sadly.

"Will you two stop that ridiculous billing and cooing!" Fabian interrupted. "We've got a line of clothes to push, and we need to get pushing right now!"

After they were gone, Gaby stared at the sofa for a long time. The indentations in the cushions spoke of their passion. The fact that those indentations were empty spoke of her loneliness. Raphael had been gone only a second and already she missed him. With another deep sigh she turned and headed for the bedroom to change her clothes.

When she walked into her office, Margie waved a sheaf of messages at her. "Richard called and so did Hamilton, plus a dozen others. Looks like it's going to be a busy day. Which call do you want to return first? Richard sounded the most impatient."

Gaby shrugged. "He always is. Let me see the other messages."

"Shall I get him on the phone?" Margie persisted.

"No, I don't want to talk to him, and before you can ask, I don't want to talk to Hamilton, either. And if John calls, I'm also not available."

"Last night must have been some night! Want to tell me about it?"

"No, I don't. But I do have a question: How did you know Raphael was at my home?"

"Well, where else would he be? Fabian came in here raging that Raphael hadn't been at his penthouse all night. It wasn't hard to put two and two together." A scarlet blush flooded Margie's face as she clapped a hand over her mouth. "Gabrielle, I'm sorry. I didn't mean that as a double entendre."

"I know you didn't. Let me get some coffee, then come into my office and tell me more about the mess with the fashion show for the dentists' wives. I thought we had everything set."

Gaby poured coffee into a fragile china cup and started into her office. After three steps she stopped so abruptly that Margie charged into her back.

"Boss, I'm sorry," Margie apologized. "I didn't mean to make you spill coffee on your new white carpeting."

"Don't worry about it; we'll clean it up later. What I want to know right now is, who's trying to turn my office into a fabric store? There must be a dozen bolts of velvet scattered around in here."

"Your decorator, who else? I told him not to leave them here, but he just fluttered his hand at me and gushed about how positively wonderful the velvet was going to look as a stage set. Then he minced out before I could stop him. His lisp drives me crazy!"

"Lisp or not, he's right. Glitter and opulence is in this season, and velvet will be the perfect background to set off the gowns I've chosen. The dentists' wives will love it. Now, bring in your pad. I want to give you a list of the models I want working the show."

Gaby glanced down at one of the messages in her

hand. "Oh, and call Nicole and tell her that until she loses those five pounds, not to waste her time or ours by asking if we have a job assignment for her."

Just as she said that, the phone rang, then the door opened and four hopeful models walked into the outer office. Gaby's hand reached for the receiver when the second line buzzed, then the third. "Looks like it's going to be a wild day!" she muttered.

Eight hours and a missed lunch later, Gaby remained at her desk, trying to untangle some final details concerning the fashion show for the dental convention. Raphael had called twice, but unfortunately her news was the same both times: Dinner would have to wait.

As she glanced through some fabric swatches, trying to decide in which order the gowns should be shown, someone knocked on the outer door of her office suite.

When she unlocked it, she found Raphael waiting outside. He grinned at her and lifted the picnic hamper up for her to see. "Even slaving business executives, wheeling and dealing in the world of high fashion, have to eat sometime."

"My noble knight returns to save the damsel a second time. I'm starving! There was no time for lunch. What did you bring, takeout chicken or hamburgers?"

"My Gabrielle, I may live in America, but that does not mean I have to eat hamburgers. And greasy fried chicken is hardly a dish fit for so beautiful a woman," he insisted, setting the hamper down on her desk.

"Whatever is in there, it smells wonderful!"

With a flourish he threw back the wicker lid. The first thing he removed was a pair of silver candlesticks, complete with candles. He glanced in distaste at her ceiling as he lit a match. "I refuse to dine with the most precious woman in my life under artificial lighting."

When the room was romantically dim, lighted only by the flickering candles, he started lifting containers out of the basket. As each emerged he explained, "To start, we have chilled vichyssoise. Sorry, but I skipped the salad: It doesn't travel well. Then for the main course we shall share coq au vin served on a rice pilaf and complemented by slivers of carrots braised in butter and basil." With an elegant flourish he whipped out the last container. "Voilá, and for dessert we have a chocolate soufflé. Finally the feast shall be crowned with this bottle of well-aged Medoc." He placed the wine bottle on her desk as he held his arms open wide. "Come, don't you think the chef deserves a kiss?"

Gaby laughed, pointing to the bottom of the hamper. "I certainly do. Move aside while I call Frank so he can take me. You forgot to take out the bill from La Louvre."

"Well"—he shrugged—"it was worth a try. This morning only wetted my appetite. I've been hungry for more kisses all day."

"Just kisses?"

"Don't ask ridiculous questions." He started advancing purposefully toward her. "You know what I want."

Gaby warded him off by thrusting a plate at him. "Here, I'm sure what you want is dinner."

"All right," he laughed, taking the china plate from her. "I know you're hungry, so I'll allow myself to be distracted . . . this time. But many more distractions and I'm going to explode."

Without really being aware of it, they rushed

131

through the meal as if hurrying toward what both knew lay ahead. It hardly did justice to the exceptional cuisine, but neither cared.

Gaby ate the last spoonful of chocolate soufflé and smiled at him. "You saved my life. I didn't realize how hungry I was."

Fascinated, Raphael watched her tongue slip out to lick the last dab of chocolate soufflé from her lips, then retreat back into her mouth. His eyes glittered with a heat so hot, Gaby knew he wished his tongue could follow, tasting the same sweetness within her mouth that she did. She smiled, deciding to inflame his desire a bit more.

With deliberately provocative strokes she let her tongue slip out again, darting into the corners of her mouth, then licking her lips, leaving them moist and inviting. Enjoying the fire she generated in his eyes as he watched her, she started to trace a fingertip over her lips with slow, tantalizing strokes. Finally her lips parted and she began sucking on her little finger.

"Gabrielle, do you know what you're doing to me?" The husky rasp of his voice thrilled her almost as much as the desire she read in the glittering blackness of his eyes.

"Of course I know. I'm doing the same thing to you that you did to me when you walked out in those black leather pants. The buyers weren't the only ones who wanted to yell 'Take it off.'"

"I wish you had. I've been living in hell these last couple of days."

She looked at him, knowing the desire burned as hotly in her eyes as in his, and not caring. She had been so long without the sensual rapture only he could give her. Resistance was gone. She wanted him. And nothing else mattered. Her body yearned

132

for his possession, yearned for the feel of his hands on her, yearned for the delicious thrusts that would send both of them to their own private paradise where sensation ruled.

A small smile touched her lips as she whispered the command that had been residing in her heart ever since she felt his lips begin to caress the back of her neck that first day he'd returned to her life.

"Take it off, Raphael. Take it all off."

With the words finally spoken, his smile lighted the room. Wanting to savor the moment, he picked up his wineglass and held it toward her in tribute: "To the most beautiful, most sexy, most wildly passionate woman in the world. To tonight and every night thereafter."

After downing the wine, one side of his mouth curled up in a rakish smile. "And now for a bed worthy of such a woman."

With deft flicks of his wrist he sent bolt after bolt of velvet cascading into a lush heap on the floor. Soft candlelight, a bed of velvet, Raphael standing before her, her office became transformed into a place of fantasy, a place out of time where the past, the present, the future, had no meaning. Slowly, Raphael walked toward her, her noble knight come to claim finally his prize.

His fingers trembled as he stripped the suit jacket from her body. Quickly the rest of her clothes followed until she stood naked before him. He devoured her with his eyes. "It's been so long," he said breathily. "You put me through hell, Gabrielle. I would dream I was holding you, making love to you. Then I'd wake up and try to reach out to you, but you were never there. It turned my nights into a place of nightmares, never dreams."

"I'm here now, Raphael."

At last a smile touched his firm lips. "Undress me, Gabrielle."

It was an order, yet so tenderly given, she didn't hesitate to comply. As she eagerly reached for his buttons he spoke the words carved into his heart: "I want to feel your hands touching me again. I want them to curl around me, to feel my power. I want them to burn away the pain of the last three years. I don't want to remember we were ever apart!"

The last of his garments fell to the floor. In the dim candlelight he looked like a magnificent Greek god. Muscles sculpted in flesh, a golden sheen to his skin—she couldn't have drawn her eyes away even if she'd wanted to. Then finally, with an urge she had no power to control, her gaze traveled downward until it rested on the source of the pleasure that would soon be hers.

When he reached for her, she begged, "Let me look at you. It's been so long," she whispered, echoing his words.

At last her hands couldn't resist the temptation any longer. Her eyes greedily followed their path as they stroked over his chest, thrilling to the remembered delight of tangling in the dark hair curling there. Her fingers descended to his narrow waist, where the feel of his flesh sent her heart pounding. Then, at last, they moved to touch the strong column she knew would soon drive her into a delirious frenzy. As her fingers curled around him, then began to stroke him, he moaned.

Quickly his fingers closed over hers, stopping her strokes. "Gabrielle, don't. I don't think I can stand much more if you touch me there. I want you too much to rush."

She smiled at the power to arouse him that she possessed. This man so many women desired be-

134

longed only to her. Trembled only for her. Said he wanted only her.

Her fingers, again free, touched his face and repeated the plea of the morning. "Love me, Raphael. Love me now."

Strong arms swept around her, lifting her high against his chest as he carried her to their bed of love. The velvet, soft and wickedly lush, welcomed her as he eased her to her back. Instead of following her down, Raphael knelt beside her.

"Gabrielle . . . my Gabrielle . . ." He repeated her name over and over as if trying to convince himself she was really lying naked in front of him, was really going to wrap her legs around him, was really finally going to ease the ache that had been his constant companion for the last three years.

He laid two fingertips against her lips, waited for her to bless them with her kiss, then began trailing them slowly down her body. They touched her swollen breasts, teasing the nipples into taut peaks, then continued their voyage. The flesh of her stomach quivered as, with butterfly-light strokes, he moved across it, then down.

Gaby's eyes closed, knowing what was coming. With no light, no sight, to distract her, she wanted to feel to its fullest every sensation he'd create. His two fingers gently parted her thighs, then entered her, sliding into the sweet moisture that told him she burned as hotly with desire as he did. Her hips rose to meet his thrust, retreat, thrust. The repeated strokes nearly drove her wild as she writhed beneath his touch. Then, when she didn't think she could stand the torment a second longer, his thumb found her.

"Raphael, please . . . please . . . ple . . ." The words faded into a soft "Ahhhhh . . ."

The exquisite pleasure brought tears, but she knew the sweetest was yet to come. She wrapped her arms tightly around him as she begged, "Please, I want you. Let me feel you inside of me . . . now!"

A second later he drove into her tenderly but hard with a passion that sucked her breath away. The explosion of their union set off a blaze within her. She burned with a thousand sparks and loved every moment of it. They had been apart too long, the desire building too hot, for a slow savoring of love. The timeless movements of desire rocked them as they moved together, seeking relief. Faster and faster, bodies damp from their passion, they clung together, each wanting to feel, to touch, to possess, every inch of the other.

With each powerful thrust of his body the spiral of sensation whirled faster within her. With each eager response he gave her more of what her body craved. The bad memories of the last three years burned away under the final fabulous blaze of their desire as finally they reached the ultimate fulfillment together.

Spent with their wild passion, the candles were sputtering low when she finally stirred. Feeling the movement, Raphael's voice sounded sadly in her ear as he whispered, "Gabrielle, I'm sorry."

CHAPTER EIGHT

Tears sprang to Gaby's eyes when she heard Raphael's words. Sorry? Why was he sorry? Had their passion not lived up to his fantasy?

In the dim candlelight she searched his eyes. "Raphael what's wrong? I don't understand. Are you sorry we made love?"

"Oh, Gabrielle, how can you ask that?" He hugged her close against the length of his naked body. "This is the moment I've waited for for so long, I still can hardly believe you are really lying in my arms."

She entwined her legs with his, drawing him closer and undulating her hips under him in a most suggestive manner. "I'll be delighted to prove this is real. Then, if you're still not convinced, we can try it over and over and over until you believe."

His response to her suggestion was immediate. And as she felt the fluttering within her begin to grow and swell, she smiled.

"Gabrielle, what you do to me!" Raphael sighed. "That's why I said I was sorry. I'd planned this for so long. I wanted it to be so wonderful. Yet, when I touched you, I wanted you so much, I couldn't wait. Instead of the slow, romantic seduction I'd planned, we came together explosively, like a match touching dynamite."

"To tell you the truth, I rather enjoyed that explosion!" Gentle hands cupped his face. "Raphael, you're a wonderful lover. You couldn't have been any better. You couldn't have satisfied me any more. It was perfect. Please believe me."

Gaby's hands left his face and began stroking his back; then they slid downward over his buttocks to find the powerful muscles of his thighs, which had always enchanted her. "We have all night to be romantic."

Her hand moved upward again with teasing strokes until she found him, robbing him of any words. All he could do was murmur her name. But he didn't have to say anything else. The wild throbbing growing harder inside her spoke more eloquently than any words he could utter.

"And what is more romantic than a bed of velvet?" She continued in a husky whisper, pulling a piece of the silken cloth about them to make a cozy, sensuous nest. As she started rubbing his body with the luxuriant fabric, she asked, "All night to be romantic, long hours of lovemaking—is that what you want? I'm here, Raphael." Her legs tightened about him. "Show me over and over how much you want me. Make me admit that when I'm in your arms, I can't say no . . . to *anything*."

Raphael found his voice at last as he began nibbling her ear. With a deep sigh he wished, "If only we had a bottle of champagne!"

The next two weeks flashed by faster than any Gaby had ever experienced. The days were filled with work. The fashion show for the wives of the dentists went splendidly. The only hitch was the velvet, that damned velvet, they'd used to dress the stage. It drove her crazy. Every time she saw it, her blood started heating up. Every time she touched it, the heat exploded into fire—a fire she would carry home each night for Raphael to satisfy in her bedroom.

Long nights filled with love, long days filled with work—Gaby should have been exhausted. Instead she glowed. She had never been happier in her life. Their passion blazed so hot, it burned through her doubts about the future. She wanted so desperately to believe they had a future together that she refused to question Raphael's vague assurances. Instead she thought only of the next time she could slip into his arms and let the world disappear.

The only thing marring her happiness was Raphael's burgeoning popularity. Every highway had a billboard featuring his picture. Magazines, television shows, newspapers—they all wanted an interview with him. But worst of all were the women. Every time she and Raphael entered a restaurant, they were mobbed as the women shoved Gaby aside to ask for his autograph or just to touch him. Once, when they tried to go to a disco, his fans had ripped off his shirt before he'd even gotten in the door. Raphael swore he didn't enjoy the attention. But what man wouldn't?

One Wednesday morning, as she waltzed into her office, humming happily to herself, Margie observed, "Whoever said you are a grouch in the morning is crazy. You're so happy, you'd light up the night."

Gaby smiled but didn't encourage the conversation. Then she looked closer at her secretary. *A cat who's just found the cream pitcher, that's what she looks like*, mused Gaby. *I wonder what she's up to.* Then she shoved the question aside. A man probably put that twinkle in her eye, but she didn't have time to listen to tales of Margie's latest conquest. Instead she asked, "Are all the plans set for the Junior League show at Bent Tree Country Club?"

"Of course they are. You always have everything planned down to the last detail. Oh, my gosh!" Margie slapped her forehead. "How could I forget? You've hit the big time. The casting agent out at dasas Colinas called and wants you to supply all the models for some big movie they're shooting there. They want to start the casting late next week. What does that commercial say, 'You've come a long way, baby'?" She paused; her excitement made her hazel eyes glow. "When can I go out and watch them shoot? I've never seen a movie being made."

Thrilled at finally breaking into the lucrative film industry, Gaby smiled. "That's great news! I've been trying to crack that market for months. And before you start pestering me, I am sure there'll be time for you to go out to the set."

Several hours later, Raphael's knock interrupted her work on the budget estimates for the film contract. She smiled a welcome at him. "Come in. I'm ready for a break. Even using the computer, it takes forever to work out these figures."

"Then the timing couldn't be better. Let's go to dinner."

Gaby glanced at her watch. "It's only three o'clock. Besides, I thought we decided not to eat out anymore. The last time I almost got trampled."

"We won't be bothered at this place, I guarantee it!" He grabbed her hand and hauled her to her feet. "Come on, all work and no play makes Gabrielle . . . ooops. I can never call you dull. Especially not after what you did to me in the shower last night. It's a wonder we didn't drown. Who

140

would have guessed you ever had such wicked thoughts."

She giggled. "You didn't seem to mind."

"What man would? Anyway, back to dinner. Hurry, we're going to be late."

"Raphael, I can't. I've got work to do."

"Margie can handle it." His eyes narrowed mischievously. "Do I have to start some ear-nibbling? When I do that, I can make you agree to *anything.*"

"I know, and it's embarrassing!"

Raphael leaned toward her, but Gaby backed away. "Okay, I'll go. My ears still haven't recovered from that ride to Howard Johnson's."

Raphael didn't let go of her hand as they entered Margie's office. "We're off," he said, giving Gaby's secretary a conspiratorial wink.

Margie straightened her shoulders. "Don't worry, I'll handle everything while you're gone."

Gaby laughed. "We're just going out to eat. I'll be back in a couple of hours."

Frank and the Mercedes were waiting in the parking garage. As they climbed in Gaby asked, "Just where is this secluded restaurant where no one will bother us?"

"Frank knows the way."

Following Raphael's suggestion, they stayed so busy talking that Gaby hardly noticed the traffic around them. Suddenly, during a lull she glanced up and frowned. "Raphael, what are we doing at Love Field? I suppose we might find some privacy here, but airport food is not my idea of heaven."

"If you can have a craving for fried clams, I can have a craving for Mexican food."

"But—"

"Frank turn there," Raphael interrupted her pro-

141

test to give the chauffeur directions. "Yes, that's right, the one on the left."

"Raphael, why are we dining on someone's private jet?" Gaby asked, staring at the gleaming white Lear jet.

"Come on, we've got a lot to do. Frank, you know what your instructions are, right?"

"Sure thing, Mr. Salvaje. I've taken care of everything." He glanced at his watch. "Better get moving. You've got only forty-five minutes."

"Raphael, will you please—"

"Sorry, Gabrielle, you heard Frank. We have only forty-five minutes."

"Forty-five minutes to do what?" she demanded.

"Up you go" was Raphael's only answer as he guided her up the steps and into the plane.

Gaby glanced around at the plush interior. Sky-blue velour seats for eight, a small bar and galley in the back—it had all the comforts of home.

But Raphael gave her no time to linger as he grabbed her hand and pulled her into the cockpit. "Sit down, my love, and be my co-pilot for a while." He winked with special meaning. "There's more than one way to 'soar' together."

"Raphael, will you please—"

"Sorry, no time. Hand me those maps in that leather box there. I've got to check our flight plan."

"Flight plan? Where are we going?"

"I told you, I'm hungry for Mexican food."

"So?"

"So, isn't it obvious? We're going to Mexico."

"Raphael, I can't. I've got a hundred things I have to do. We've got a fashion show for the Junior League coming up, and—"

"And Margie's going to handle everything. She said you have everything so efficiently planned, a

142

child could run things. She's even packed your luggage for the trip. So you relax. The next five days are ours."

Her lips parted with a protest, then closed as the delicious prospect of spending five days alone with him in Mexico won over her feeling of responsibility to her job. Besides, he was right: All the plans were set for the fashion show Friday. And Margie shouldn't have any trouble handling the commentary. Still, one thing bothered her.

"But, Raphael, renting a jet? Isn't this awfully expensive? And, now that I think of it, when did you learn to fly?"

He grinned at her as he flipped on the radio to check the weather reports. "I had to do something to fill my lonely hours after you left me, didn't I? But knowing how you feel about my driving, I decided you'd feel safer with another pilot actually handling the controls. He'll be here in a little while."

She shook her head. "Racing cars, flying jets . . . don't you ever do anything safe?"

"Playing it safe makes life boring. Now, hand me those navigational maps."

"I think I'd trade boring for dangerous anytime," Gaby muttered under her breath as she bent over the leather box. "So, we're not going to be alone."

"We are . . . and we aren't." He commented with irritating vagueness. He reached over and squeezed her hand. "Love, I'll explain everything once we're in the air. But right now I've got a lot of preflight checking to do."

"You're driving me crazy!" she protested.

His teeth flashed in a grin. "I plan to do a lot of that in the next five days."

Before she could comment, a man opened the door to the cockpit.

"Good, you're here," Raphael greeted the other pilot. "Gabrielle, I'm sorry, but you're going to have to move back to that jump seat until we take off."

After the pilot, William, introduced himself, he requested clearance from the tower.

A few minutes later Dallas lay in glittering splendor beneath their wings as William banked sharply to the southwest, then leveled out on their flight path.

"William, be a pal and flip on the automatic pilot. Gabrielle and I would like to be alone for a while. I'll call you when we're ready to land."

The other man grinned in understanding as he headed toward the passenger compartment.

"All right, we're alone. Now, please, can I have some answers?" she begged as she returned to the co-pilot's seat beside Raphael. "Where are we going? And *why* are we going?"

"We're going so I can make love to you over and over again. Remember Saint-Tropez?" The fire in his eyes as he looked at her ignited an equally hot blaze within hers as he continued: "I want our reunion blessed with the same moon shining down on us as we make love under the stars. I want the same sound of waves crashing against the shore when I take you in my arms. I want to swim naked with you in the ocean like we did then. I want those memories merged with reality."

Her hand came up to her breast as if she were trying to keep her heart from bursting: She was that filled with joy. "Raphael, what can I say to answer so beautiful a thought."

"Just say you love me. I need no other words."

144

She gazed at him and spoke from her soul. "I love you Raphael."

"I know." He stroked her cheek with a fingertip. "We're going to celebrate our love in Ixtapa on the Mexican Riviera. It's small, secluded, without the hordes of tourists in places like Acapulco. It's the perfect place to mix business and pleasure—lots and lots of pleasure!"

"What business?"

He grinned. "They have to shoot that cover for *Gentlemen's Quarterly* somewhere. Why not in a romantic place like Ixtapa? I came up with the idea, and Fabian sold it to the magazine. It's working out great. Niko owns the hotel the crew will be staying at and where we will be doing some of the shooting, so he's pleased about the publicity. We're using this jet in one of the shots, so that's deductible. *You're* even making money on the deal."

"How did *I* get involved in this?"

"You don't think I'd let them use anybody else's models, do you?"

"Raphael, it sounds wonderful!" Gaby sighed. "Five days with just the sun, the sand, and you. I haven't had a real vacation since I got back from Europe. I've always loved the sea. The sound of waves breaking does something to me."

"I remember." He smiled at the memory. "You always were a little wilder in Saint-Tropez than in Paris. Why do you think I thought of Ixtapa? I love it when you're wild!"

A burst of laughter from the cabin reminded Gaby they weren't alone. "I'm not very excited about sharing you with anyone, even for a minute. Who am I going to have to battle for your attention?"

145

"The three models Fabian picked out, the photographer, Fabian . . . and a surprise."

"Another surprise. You're really spoiling me."

"I know, but I love to do it. Look down: We're flying over the Sierra Madre mountains. It won't be long now before we can land at Zihuatanejo."

"You mean Ixtapa doesn't have an airport?" The palms of Gaby's hands broke out in a cold sweat as she suddenly realized they'd have to drive to the resort.

"No, love, I'm afraid it doesn't." Raphael curled his fingers about Gaby's arm to reassure her. "But it will be all right. I promise."

Her stomach churned and bubbled at the thought of riding in a car without Frank. It fought with the fabulous prospect of spending five days with Raphael. She tried to tell herself that five days in paradise with the man she loved was worth any sacrifice, but the fear blunted her happiness.

They flew over one last ridge of mountains, and Gaby gasped when she saw the blue Pacific stretching outward from the miles and miles of glistening white sand beaches. With William back at the controls they began their descent into Zihuatanejo. She could see the waves below rolling in, the palm trees swaying in the warm breezes, and the splash of tropical flowers brightening every corner.

Raphael waved his hand over the scene spread out below their wings. "Our own private paradise. There's just one thing wrong: The water isn't blue enough. I liked the way the sea along the Côte d' Azur matched the azure of your eyes." His expression softened. "I will take you back there someday, my Gabrielle. I promise."

After they'd landed at the tiny airport in the fishing village of Zihuatanejo, Gaby unbuckled her seat belt and started to rise. "No, wait. We've still got some postflight business to finish up here while William checks us in with Customs."

After five minutes of stowing maps and checking gauges, he said, "Okay, everything should be set now. Are you ready to find paradise, my Gabrielle?"

"I think anywhere I was with you would seem like paradise," she whispered.

"Gabrielle, if you keep looking at me like that, I won't even wait until we get to our villa before I make you mine."

"Our villa? I thought you said—"

"I promised you we'd find privacy here. And a big hotel is not very private." He held up his hand. "And before you berate my extravagance, the villa also belongs to Niko. He's doing a lot of heavy investing in the resorts along the coast and wanted a private place to stay when he came over here on business."

Gaby's eyes widened in happy surprise when she stepped down onto the concrete of the runway. "Raphael!" she whirled around to hug him. "Now everything *is* perfect!"

"Howdy, ma'am." Frank doffed his cowboy hat in welcome. "Sorry I couldn't round up a Mercedes." He gestured to the battered Cadillac at his side. "This is the best I could do out here in the sticks."

Raphael looked at the happy glow on her face and smiled. "I told Fabian there would be no filming until tomorrow. So come, love, the sea awaits."

Niko's villa was down the coast from Ixtapa on its own private secluded cove. Gleaming white in the hot tropical sun, it beckoned to them, promising the privacy they both craved. As Frank brought the big Cadillac smoothly to a stop, Raphael said, "We

147

won't need you until tomorrow morning at about nine."

The interior of the villa remained serenely cool against the glare of the sun. Painted tiles underfoot, stark white walls softened with native weavings, comfortable rattan furniture—it was the perfect retreat from the world. With Raphael's arm about her waist, she snuggled against him as they explored their home for the next five days. No other sounds echoed but their footsteps. Obviously they were alone.

Finally he stopped at a set of soaring double arches. Inside the room a long wooden table hosted an inviting buffet of Mexican food. "You see, I'm a man of my word. I invited you to dinner, and here it is." He winked at her. "The cook's gone home. So has everyone else." Raphael held out his arm to her. "My love, shall we dine?"

Guacamole, tostadas heaped with chili and cheese, gazpacho, sour-cream enchiladas—everything looked so tempting, Gaby didn't know where to start.

Raphael inhaled deeply as he took the cover off the pot of *arroz con pollo.* "Chicken and rice: It reminds me of home. This is what we'd have every Sunday." He spooned some onto her plate. "Try it and dream of Spain."

Gaby wiped up the last dab of guacamole with her tortilla and popped it into her mouth, then licked her lips. "I think guacamole is what I missed most when I was modeling. It has so many calories, it's sinful."

Raphael chuckled. "A lot of things around here are sinful . . . and we're going to enjoy every one of them." He pushed his plate back, then reached

148

into his pocket. "Come here, Gabrielle. I have something for you."

When she was nestled on his lap, he handed her a flat velvet box. "Oh, Raphael." She sighed, when she opened the box and saw the diamond unicorn dangling from a gold chain. The candlelight glittering off the hundreds of facets almost blinded her as she protested, "But you shouldn't have. It's too expensive."

His carefree laughter filled the room. "Ah, my practical Gabrielle, don't you realize nothing is too expensive when it's for you. I saw it and knew you had to have it." He kissed the back of her neck, then fastened the necklace into place. "Don't you see, that's why we're so good together: I'm impulsive; you're always cautious. I'm extravagant; you've probably got the first dollar you earned. Together we're the perfect combination."

"Opposites attract—is that your theory?" she asked with a smile.

"You've got to admit, it sure seems to be working out that way."

Before she could stop the words, her concern slipped out. "Yes, but how long will that be true, Raphael? Do we have a future?"

"Gabrielle, everything will work out. I promise."

"How?"

Raphael sighed. "Just trust me, love. As soon as this most-eligible-bachelor nonsense is finished, everything will be perfect."

Gaby gazed at him. No answers, just vague promises. Could she go on living one day at a time? Raphael gave her no other choice. Yet, the uncertainties continued to gnaw at the edges of her happiness.

Raphael's finger smoothed away her worried

149

frown. "The moon's up, love. The ocean's waiting. Let the water make us forget there is any world outside this villa." He smiled. "Then it will be paradise."

When he looked at her that way, nothing else mattered. He became her world, her paradise. One smile from him and the tingling of excitement started within her, giving promises of the long moonlit hours ahead.

A teasing shrug sent the edge of her boat-necked blouse slipping over her bare shoulder. "How can we go swimming? I didn't bring a suit."

Raphael lifted her off his lap and set her on her feet. "The moon will never tell."

A racking shudder shook him when she stood before him with nothing on but the diamond unicorn. No clothes shielded the evidence of his blatant desire; yet, he didn't reach for her. Instead he closed his eyes a long moment to gather control. When he opened them again, the fire still kindled but the blaze had died.

"Nothing is going to spoil the beauty of this night. I am going to love you, my Gabrielle, until you beg for mercy."

Gaby swallowed, trying to control her own desire. "Like a vanquished army?" she whispered.

"My love, the surrender will be sweeter than anything you've ever known," Raphael vowed, taking her hand.

The brilliant moonlight turned the waves into a sea of diamonds that glittered almost as brightly as the ones about her neck. Hand and hand, they walked into the surf. As the sea washed over them Raphael took her in his arms. It was as he'd promised. Waves crashing around them, the moonlight shining down to bless them, the bed of soft sand awaiting them—all reality merged into his embrace as he took her into his arms.

The sea spray coated her lips. Carefully he licked the salt away; then with a sigh her lips parted for him to take his pleasure, a pleasure she knew would be hers as well. Under the water she could feel the power of his passion pressing between her legs, begging to take its own pleasure. Back and forth, the rubbing strokes teased her, but when she arched her back, trying to capture the power for herself, he wouldn't enter her. Instead the delicious torment went on and on until her heartbeat pounded so loudly in her ears, it covered the sound of the surf.

Even the cool waters of the Pacific couldn't sip the heat from her skin as Raphael continued to tease her. Even when she wrapped her legs around him, desperate to escape the torment firing hotter and hotter inside her, he refused. Instead the strokes began again, prolonging her sweet agony. Back and forth, back and forth with velvet thrusts, touching her where she throbbed, yet always slipping away from total possession. Gaby could do nothing but moan his name as chills of passion streaked through her, enflaming every nerve, always returning to the core of her soul, now burning with need for him.

Finally, when she didn't think she could endure another moment, she felt him enter her with a driving lunge that sent waves of pleasure rocketing through her, bringing her to a shuddering crest. And even as the release pulled a soft moan from her lips, the pleasure began building again.

Lying back in his arms, letting the sea be her bed as she arched against him, the passion mounted. In and out, faster and faster, rhythmically he created a symphony of sensation within her. Echoing the beat of the sea, the internal music grew, swelled, consumed her with the power of a Beethoven overture. Then, when she thought she couldn't stand any more, the strokes slowed, touching her softly like the notes of a flute, only to swell once again in a crescendo that engulfed every sense.

Over and over again he brought her almost to the brink of paradise, only to leave her a heartbeat short as he started building the passion anew. Obviously determined to control his desire this time, he refused to let her touch him. "No, Gabrielle, not yet," he whispered. When she pulled herself against him, wanting to drive his possession deeper, he quieted her with a caress. With teasing strokes he withdrew until her helpless moan of "Raphael, no!" sent him plunging back to start the symphony over from the beginning. The waves crashing around them grew wilder, mirroring the wild passion building within them.

Finally, in desperation Gaby wrapped her arms around his neck and captured his mouth with hers. As her tongue plunged hungrily in and out of his mouth, hitting the same rhythm as his thrusts, his control snapped. Together they rode the waves, rocking together, each pulling the other higher until one final wild drive into her body brought an exquisite end to their passion.

Gaby lay weakly in his arms as Raphael carried her toward shore. Even if he'd asked her to walk, she didn't think her legs would have carried her. Into the villa, up the stairs, to the cool tiles of the bathroom, he went. Then, in a bathtub large enough for two, he sank beside her into the warm water. After gently washing the salt from her body, her long hair, her eyelashes, he kissed her. "Didn't I tell you we'd find paradise?"

CHAPTER NINE

Too early the next day, the real world intruded into their paradise as Frank's toots interrupted their breakfast. Gaby sighed. "Don't tell me it's nine already?"

"I'm afraid so, my love." Raphael took the last sip of his coffee. "Come with me to the photo session, please."

"You'd better believe I will. You didn't think I'd leave you alone with three beautiful models, did you?"

"Gabrielle, after last night, how could you doubt that you're the only woman in the world for me."

Still, even with all his assurances, Gaby felt a twinge when her models draped themselves adoringly over him for a shot. Pictures were taken in the swimming pool of the hotel; more were shot on the beach; then with Raphael dressed in a tuxedo, they returned to Zihuatanejo for shots by the Lear jet.

She was standing behind the cameraman when he shouted, "Okay, that's a wrap for this locale. The next set will be out on the catamaran."

Gaby smiled when she saw Raphael tugging on his bow tie, trying to loosen it. She started toward him but stopped when Fabian rushed up to talk to him.

Obviously whatever Fabian said to Raphael was

good news, because when he finished, a delighted smile flashed across Raphael's face and he clapped the other man on the back as if to say, "Job well done."

"What was all that about?" she asked when he joined her.

"A surprise," he answered evasively.

"Another surprise!" She beamed happily. "Come on, Raphael, tell me what it is. Secrets always make me green with curiosity."

"I'll tell you this much: it has something to do with our future."

"Our future? Go on."

"That's all the hint you're going to get, my nosy Gabrielle."

"Raphael, please tell me what's going on," she pleaded, wanting to know what had happened to affect their future.

"Look, Gabrielle, there are still some details to work out, so why don't we wait and discuss the surprise when we get back to Dallas, okay? And don't look like that: Pouting isn't becoming," he teased, kissing her lightly.

Before she could press him, Fabian joined them. "Hey, those models of yours are dyn-a-mite! The crew from *GQ* are ecstatic over the pictures they're getting. This is going to make you bigger than ever!" he bragged.

"I'm not sure . . ." Raphael began, but Fabian hurried on.

"Your idea of using a private jet was pure inspiration. What better symbol of the rich life, eh?" He poked Raphael in the ribs. "Now, let's get back to the hotel so you can change into some of Jean-Claude's sportswear. They want some shots of you and the girls out on the catamaran with the tropical

154

sun setting behind you. You know, sailing off into the sunset and all that kind of stuff. Hey, but what do I care? It sells."

"You go ahead in the truck. Frank will drive us," Raphael suggested, dismissing him.

Back at the hotel, Raphael captured her hand as they walked slowly through the lush tropical gardens surrounding Niko's resort. He stopped and plucked a flaming red hibiscus from a bush, then tucked it behind her ear. "There, now everyone will know you're taken."

"Are you sure you've got it behind the right ear?" she teased. "You could be telling everyone I'm available."

"Like hell you are!"

The depth of possession in his voice brought a blush to her face. "I *am* available," she murmured, "but only to you."

His hand swept beneath the heavy fall of her hair to capture her neck. As he bent toward her to confirm her confession the PA blasted to life. *"Señorita O'Shea, Señorita O'Shea, teléfono para usted. Señorita O'Shea . . ."*

"Oh, no!" she whispered, frowning.

"Do you suppose we can pretend we didn't hear that?" he asked hopefully.

"No, you know as well as I do that Margie wouldn't disturb me if it wasn't an emergency."

Several irritating clicks and clacks later, Margie's worried voice finally come on the line. "Gabrielle, I'm so sorry to bother you, but I didn't know what else to do?"

"All right, calm down and tell me what's the trouble."

"It's about the show tomorrow. Six of the seven models you'd planned to use are sick. Two of them

155

are in the hospital, and with the three you've got down there, we're stuck."

"Six out of seven? How in the world did that happen?" Gaby asked as she covered the phone and explained to Raphael, "Trouble with the show tomorrow."

"It's Valentine's fault. You know how she's always preaching about that health food restaurant she likes. Well, she talked a bunch of our girls into trying it with her. They all came down with ptomaine. Only Anna's still on her feet. She went out for a hamburger. I don't know what to do."

For a moment a sigh that reached all the way into her heart was Gaby's only answer. Then she said, "Okay, Margie, I'll be on the first plane out of here. I should get to Dallas sometime early in the morning. Set up an audition for nine o'clock. Call anyone you can think of. Start with Nicole—at least she has experience—then get those four who came into the office the other day. Thank goodness the clothes this year aren't tightly fitted."

A deep sadness touched her as she dropped the receiver on the hook, then turned to Raphael. "I'm sorry, but there isn't—"

He bent to kiss her, stilling her words. When he pulled away he admitted, "I know there isn't anything else you can do, but I can tell you one thing: The moon, the ocean, and I, are going to be very lonely!" His sigh echoed the pain of hers. "Let's go find Frank. I know you'll want him to return with you."

The lights of Dallas had seemed so bright when she'd left them the day before. Now, in the gray predawn Texas light, they looked dreary. Or maybe they looked that way because that was the way she

156

felt. Gaby rubbed her tired eyes as she closed the magazine and buckled her seat belt. "Too bad paradise didn't last," she muttered to herself.

Eight hours later Gaby laid her head against the back of the seat as Frank drove them toward the office. "What is it they say? 'Out of the winds of adversity blows some good.' We pulled the show off, and two of those models you found, Margie, were good enough to sign. I've got a bottle of wine chilling. We'll toast to the excellent job you did," she complimented her secretary. "Then I'm going home to bed."

The newspapers were stacked neatly on her desk as Gaby headed toward the concealed bar. Suddenly one headline caught her attention and she skidded to a halt.

"Gabrielle, what is it?" Margie demanded, putting a concerned hand on her arm. "You look like you've just seen a ghost."

Gaby forced the words through tight lips: "Margie, I want to be alone."

"Sure, sure, whatever you say," she agreed, quickly backing out of the room, then closing the door behind her.

Tears of pain blurred the headline as Gaby stared at it; yet, to her regret she could still read the words: RAPHAEL SALVAJE TEAMS WITH FERRARI TO DRIVE THE DALLAS GRAND PRIX.

In her mind, terrifying memories of the fiery crash at Monte Carlo mixed in a horrible montage with scenes from their own accident. Fear for the safety of the man she loved gripped her in savage jaws as she thought of Raphael racing. Somewhere deep within her she realized that fear was irrational, but she had no power to control the feeling as her heart cried over and over *How could he?*

157

Raphael hadn't changed. He'd never change. Danger would always be his first love. How could she have been so stupid to hope? Yet, even as her thoughts raged, some thread within her was not surprised. In fact, that tiny part of her had almost expected something like this. Was it happening as she'd feared? Raphael had gotten what he'd wanted. He'd seduced her back into his bed. So was he now off to find some new challenge? Never satisfied, always pushing fate to the limit—that was Raphael. It made no sense to love a man like that . . . but she did.

Over the next twenty-four hours Gaby fell into a world of misery as her dreams, her hopes, crumbled about her. She couldn't sleep. She couldn't eat. By eight o'clock the next evening, when her doorbell rang, she could hardly summon the energy to answer it.

Raphael was standing outside, a brilliant smile on his tanned face. "Surprise!" he laughed. "I rushed things through so we could—"

In one motion Gaby slammed the door in his face, then clapped her hands over her ears as he started pounding.

"Gabrielle, open this door! What's wrong? Gabrielle, listen to me!"

His voice, softened with that Spanish accent she adored, drove the pain so deeply into her heart, she didn't know if she'd ever feel anything again.

"Gabrielle, open this door or I'm going to call the police."

What good would delaying the inevitable do? The good-byes might as well be said now. She pushed a strand of hair out of her face, then double-knotted her robe before turning toward the pounding. With legs feeling as if they were dragging hundred-pound weights, Gaby went to the door and opened it.

"Gabrielle, why did you slam the door? Are you sick? You look—"

"I look exactly the way I feel." Her voice threatened to crack, but she steadied it as she grabbed the damning newspaper. As she threw it at him she cried, "Thanks for the surprise! It made my day!"

Raphael caught the paper. His eyes scanned the headline and he frowned. "Gabrielle, I meant to tell you when we got back from Ixtapa."

"Was this what Fabian told you about that made you so excited?"

"Yes, their regular driver broke a leg waterskiing, of all things. And since they knew I drove in Europe and we already have a publicity link through Jean-Claude, they asked me to take his place. It's a great opportunity!"

"Sure, it's a great opportunity to have another crash!" Even the barest thought of that happening brought such a stab of pain, she couldn't bear to look at him. Blinding tears stung her eyes as she turned away. "Raphael, go. Just go."

"I'm not going anywhere until we've talked this out," he insisted firmly, shutting the door.

A deep sadness scarred her voice as she asked, "What's there to talk about? Nothing's changed. You're still the same man I left in France. You have to be the center of attention, don't you? First, when you were on the soccer team, and now as a sex symbol to millions of women. A Ferrari, a penthouse—you've even got the same types of expensive toys you had back then. But that's not enough. Oh, no, now it's driving in the Dallas Grand Prix. When will you grow up?"

159

"Damn it, Gabrielle, I *am* grown up. Remember Ixtapa."

Driven by her fear, she lashed out at him.

"Being a good lover doesn't mean you're a man."

The instant the words were out of her mouth, the guilt stabbing through her brought more tears. How could she have said that to Raphael? How could she have hurt him like that? She didn't feel that way about him. Yet, the thought of him driving frightened her so much, she struck back out of choking anxiety.

Raphael recoiled, almost as if she hit him; then his chin became set. "Gabrielle, someday you'll understand. You may not believe this, but driving in the Grand Prix is the most adult thing I've ever done. And I'm doing it for us, for our future."

"Our future? How can we have a future if you're not here? Raphael, your driving almost killed us in France; now you're deliberately risking your life again, and for what? The thrill of going faster than anyone else? Those are little-boy games."

"That's not why I'm doing it. I'm doing it for us," he repeated. "You must believe that!"

Her eyes searched his, trying to understand. "How, Raphael? Tell me how driving in that race will help us?"

"They're paying me a lot of money to drive. That can buy the future I want for us."

"*Money?* You're doing this for *money?*" she demanded in disbelief. "We don't need money. You have your job with Jean-Claude. Besides, my agency's been successful. I've got all the money we'd ever need. Why can't you—"

"Gabrielle, you know I could never live off the woman I love. There is an old Spanish proverb that says, 'There are some things a man must do to be a

160

man.' This is one of those things. Be patient. You will just have to trust me when I say this is important to our future. After the race I'll explain everything. I promise."

Fresh tears burned her eyes as she sadly shook her head. "Why should I believe any of your promises? You *promised* you'd never drive professionally again."

"I know, but if you'll just let me explain, I—"

"No, Raphael, I'm tired of your explanations that explain nothing. And I'm tired of being patient. All it's gotten me is vague promises that don't mean anything." She wiped the tears away with the back of her hand, then sadly admitted, "I'm not even angry at you, just at myself. I should have expected this. You haven't changed. And dear God, I'm fool enough to love you."

His hands reached out toward her, but she backed away quickly. "No, Raphael, don't touch me. I don't think I could stand it if . . ." She swallowed the words, not wanting to admit her weakness. Even now she knew if he held her, if he kissed her, she wouldn't have the strength to end it.

She turned away and walked to the window. "Raphael, go—go to your damned Ferrari. I hope it keeps you warm at night!"

She stiffened when she felt his hands close over her arms. "Gabrielle, I *have* to drive in this race. And whether you believe this or not, I *am* doing it for you, my love."

"Don't call me that! You know how I feel about cars. If you really did love me, you wouldn't be doing this."

"It's because I do love you that I am," he vowed. His hands tightened as he begged, "Gabrielle, please, I want you to be there for me."

The fear, her ever-present companion, threatened to strangle her as she whispered, "Raphael, I can't. You know I can't!"

"You must. I am racing for you. Do this for me, please."

She felt him slide something into the pocket of her robe.

"There's your ticket. The race is next Sunday. I know you can't be rational right now about my driving, but think about it this week. Just because you're afraid doesn't mean I am. I'll be all right, I promise. Gabrielle, be there—be there for me."

"Be there to watch them possibly pull you from a wreck? How can you ask that of me?"

"Gabrielle, don't—don't torture yourself. You must trust in our love. It will protect me."

"No," she whispered as he dropped his hands and turned to leave. As the door shut she sobbed, "No! Dear God, no!"

The next week Gaby sank deeper and deeper into her living hell. Raphael called, but she refused to talk to him. She'd go to the office, then sit for hours staring at the corner where they'd made love. And she found no peace at home with the sofa on which he'd held her and calmed her terror on the night of the accident. Even the Mercedes haunted her with memories of the desire he'd stirred within her on their ride to the restaurant. But worst of all was her bed. Alone at night, she couldn't keep Raphael from entering her dreams, and she'd wake up shaking—and not from fear.

How could he do this to her? She prided herself on being sane and sensible, but with Raphael she'd been so wrong. *Forget him, forget him, forget him,* her mind ordered. But her heart couldn't.

The more she tried to force him out of her mind,

the more firmly he resided there. It didn't make any sense, but who said logic had anything to do with love? Love—yes, that was what she felt for Raphael. She knew that with every fiber of her soul. She still loved him and probably always would. And in his way she was sure Raphael loved her, but just like three years ago, he didn't love her enough. If he did, he wouldn't be driving in that damned race!

Time after time Gaby pulled the ticket out of her pocket, shuddered, and shoved it back in. There was no power on earth that would make her go to that race. Just the thought of Raphael behind the same type of wheel that had killed Pepe made her tremble. She tried to separate her irrational fears from her true feelings, but they were so intertwined, it seemed impossible.

Each day ticked away like a metronome of doom. There was no escape. The television, the radio, dozens of billboards, touted the race. And, thanks to Fabian, almost every announcement included Raphael's name. Every time she heard it, it felt as though a little piece of her died.

Finally, Sunday arrived. Gaby planned to sleep late. She awoke at five A.M. Work—maybe that would help, she decided, desperate to find some way to stop thinking about Raphael and the race. She pulled the computer printout of her monthly expenses from her briefcase . . . and saw nothing.

"Damn him!" she muttered, tossing the papers aside. "Why couldn't I fall in love with a nice dull accountant!"

He filled her thoughts. He filled her heart. *I can't watch him race. I just can't! But what if . . . ? Could I live with myself if something happened to him and I wasn't there?* She trembled with fear of watching the race. She shook with fear of missing it.

Finally she found some strength as his words returned: *Trust in our love. It will protect me.*

Without being aware that she'd even reached a decision, she reached for the phone to call Frank.

Even before they got to the racetrack, the sound assaulted them as the racing cars took their warmup laps. The whine of the supercharged engines screeching around corners, then roaring down the straightaways, deafened her as Frank pulled the car to a stop by the gate.

The surging mob of people carried Gaby along toward the grandstands. With each step the noise grew louder. Like no other sound in the world, the turbo engines screamed through each shifting of gears. Her hands clenched. It was a sound of her nightmares, a sound reminding her of another day, another race, a fiery crash that took the life of a friend. Her steps faltered as a shiver of dread slithered up her spine, but she didn't stop.

She must have looked helplessly confused because one of the ushers came over to her. "Can I help you find your seat, ma'am?"

Without a word Gaby handed him her ticket. "Wow, you sure are lucky, lady. You get to sit in the Ferrari team box! You'll have a perfect view of the whole track."

Instead of delight, that news brought a frown. She didn't want to see the whole racetrack. She wasn't really sure she wanted to see any of the track at all. But she'd come this far. There was no going back.

A babble of Italian greeted her as the usher showed her into the box-seat area directly in front of the Ferrari pits. To her vast relief, when she sat down the whine of the engines quieted as the practice runs finished. Her ears still rang with the noise as a bright red car, built so low that it hugged the

164

ground, pulled into the pit area and stopped. Like ants swarming, the crew hurried to surround it, filling the fuel tank, checking the tires, talking to the driver. She strained forward. There were two Ferraris racing; was this Raphael?

Finally a burly crew member moved aside, and Gaby's heart pounded as Raphael pulled off his helmet, and instead of seeing his face, she saw only the fire-protective hood, obscuring his features. Like the blow of a sledgehammer the hood conjured up all her fears of a crash. It took every ounce of willpower she possessed not to run screaming from the box.

With a familiar gesture Raphael shoved the hood back, and at last she could see his face. She expected him to be ecstatic, anticipating the race, but when he turned toward the stands a deep frown marred his forehead. He hungrily searched the seats in the box; then that familiar smile, the one that always made her heart turn over, flashed across his face when he saw her. As the public-address system blasted to life, calling the drivers to the starting mark, Raphael touched his gloved fingers to his lips and flipped her a kiss before pushing his helmet back into place.

Low, throbbing with energy, the cars revved at the starting line. Even at a distance she felt their power, a power she knew could thrill . . . or destroy. No! She wasn't going to think about that. *Believe,* her heart begged, *believe in Raphael's words: "Our love will protect me."* She clung to the thought like a magic talisman.

Except for those terrifying moments of their crash, Gaby had never experienced fear like that which she felt watching the starter raise his gun. The bang felt like a spear driving into her heart as the machines roared down the first straightaway. The bright red of the Ferrari team was easy to spot as the cars completed the first lap. The team's number-one car was in the pole position. Raphael held sixth.

There were times she thought she couldn't stand another minute as Raphael used a wide corner to slingshot past the number-five Lotus. She chewed her fingernails down to the quick; she twisted and untwisted her hands until they were bruised; yet, her eyes never left him. Even when one of the Porsches crashed into the barrel barrier right in front of the grandstand, she didn't look away. Her only reaction was to say a silent prayer of thanks as the driver walked away from the crash, and then she added another prayer to her already long list for Raphael.

Lap after lap, around the twists and turns of the course, the cars sped by. On the back straightaway Raphael made a daring maneuver that sucked the breath from her lungs as he passed the bright yellow Renault Elf to take over third. Jockeying for position, fending off attacks, the race went on. Car after car went out, but the top five kept racing.

A dozen emotions battled within her as she watched Raphael complete each lap. How could she love a man who embraced danger like a favorite mistress? Yet, she did. How could she dream of a future with someone obviously no more ready to settle down than he had been three years ago? Yet, she did. How could Raphael touch something within her heart no other man had ever even come close to? Yet, he did. The questions droned on endlessly; the answers remained elusive.

Only one certainty remained in her heart: She

loved Raphael. After that, nothing else seemed to matter.

Suddenly the crowd surged to its feet as the starter signaled the final lap. With Ferraris in the first and third positions and a Porsche between, the lead cars tore down the back straightaway. Raphael challenged the Porsche, but the more experienced driver cut off his attempt. With a jaunty wave of his checkered flag, the starter greeted the first place Ferrari and the second-place Porsche as they crossed the finish line. Then to her surprise Gaby found herself on her feet yelling wildly with excitement as Raphael flashed across the finish line, taking third.

The exhilarated thrill shooting through her body at that moment was something she'd never experienced before. Without even being aware of it, that thrill burned away a lot of painful memories. She'd enjoyed watching Raphael challenge fate . . . and win!

Then, like the last pieces of a jigsaw puzzle falling into place, she understood. The whiff of danger, the daring, the grasping all that life could give, were part of the reason she loved Raphael. It had been like that from the first moment she saw him score a goal on the soccer field. The aura of excitement appealed not just to her passion but directly to her soul.

Raphael completed her as she completed him. She was conservative, often too cautious. He never was. Where she was timid, he dared. She had always claimed to dislike that part of him. How could she not realize that that was part of his allure, part of the reason she loved him with such intensity? Together they made a perfect pair.

Somewhere deep inside she must have known

this or she would never have welcomed him back into her life. She hadn't been a fool to love Raphael: He was the perfect man to make her happy. Her instincts had known it from the beginning. It was her common sense that had refused to see. Now she knew there had always been more depth to their relationship than she'd imagined, only she hadn't realized it. Raphael had. He'd said she was the only woman in the world for him, and he was the only man for her. That was what he'd meant by saying they were destined to meet, destined to love. At that moment, embracing that destiny, she felt happier than she'd ever been in her life.

Lost in that trance of happiness, she hardly realized someone was tapping her on the arm. *"Signorina,* there is to be a *grandioso* celebration in the garage area. You are a friend of Raphael's, no? You must come." He tapped his chest proudly in a gesture reminding her of Jean-Claude. "I, Riccardo Fabi, would be honored to escort you." He held out his arm in a courtly way. "But we must hurry. Already I see a crowd heading that way."

The sound of champagne bottles, rapidly popping like machine guns, greeted Gaby as she and Riccardo walked into the garage. After he charged off to get her a glass of champagne, Gaby anxiously began to search through the packed crowd of people for the one person who filled her heart with such love, she thought it might burst. Finally she saw Raphael standing in the middle of a group of adoring women. Even the black smudge of grease on his cheek couldn't detract from his devastating appeal, an appeal made even sweeter for her upon finally understanding the unique love she bore for him.

As she gazed at him across the garage, warm

urges began to flow through her body. She wanted desperately to be in his arms, to tell him what she'd discovered about herself, to talk of the future, and finally to love. But they couldn't do that in a mob of people. She needed long hours alone with him, and yet, she knew he couldn't leave the party. Suddenly a happy smile touched her lips as she decided what she would do. Her smile widened: She knew her plan was one surprise he'd love. Turning, she walked quickly out of the garage.

CHAPTER TEN

A private elevator took Gaby up to Raphael's pent-house. With the key he'd given her she let herself in. As the soft lights flooded the living room she smiled, knowing how surprised and pleased he'd be when he came home and found her waiting for him. The room out of a decorator's dream enthralled her every time she entered it. She walked around, lov-ingly touching his possessions. Plush carpet of the richest forest green muffled her steps as she walked toward the rough fieldstone fireplace. Closing her eyes, Gaby dreamed of long winter nights snuggled in Raphael's arms in front of a crackling fire. That pleasant thought stirred other, even more pleasant thoughts. Knowing the pleasure to be given and received once he arrived home tempted her to-ward his bedroom.

It reminded her even more of a movie set than the living room. Elevated on a dais, a massive oaken bed, with columns soaring to the ceiling, dominated the room. But it was the small table beside it that captured and held all her attention. A dozen snap-shots of her, all memories of times they'd spent together in Europe, resided there in silver frames. It thrilled her every time she saw them. Three years and still he'd kept them. Her smile softened as she picked one up and gazed at it, remembering the happiness of the day he'd taken it. And now that exquisite happiness was to be hers again. Only this time she prayed it would last forever.

Hugging that thought to her heart brought a surge of warmth as she wandered into the bathroom. For a moment she just stood there. "As I always said, this is fit for a sultan," she said laughingly to herself, glancing from the huge marble whirlpool bath in the center of the room, to the walls of mirrors, then up. She laughed again as the mirrored ceiling suddenly inspired a deliciously wicked thought.

"Mirrors, get ready to watch some fun!" she murmured, giving the tap a twist. Quickly she slipped out of her clothes, then sank down into the swirling bubbles. The heat of the water couldn't match the heat building within her as she thought of Raphael's passionate reaction to finding her naked, waiting in his bath.

An hour later Gaby's smile was gone. Where was Raphael? Surely the party was over by now. Stepping out of the tub, she looked down at her wrinkled fingertips and frowned. "So much for romping in the whirlpool. Any longer in that water and all of me would have turned into a prune."

A silk robe, one of Jean-Claude's designs, hung on the back of the door. She wrapped it around herself and knotted the belt. It trailed the floor as she walked back through his bedroom and on into the living room. Some instinct—maybe the hope that she'd be able to see his approaching headlights—led her to the balcony.

The lights of Dallas, sparkling like diamonds, sprawled below, but she didn't see their beauty as the thoughts she'd been trying to ignore finally refused to be quiet any longer. Why didn't he come?

Had she driven him away by refusing to trust him when he vowed they had a future? Had her anger over him racing again made him give up on their relationship? The scene in the garage haunted her. Was he with another woman? Was that why he hadn't returned to the penthouse? An hour later she still had no answers.

Weary of waiting, Gaby returned to the living room. Like a deflated balloon, her happiness evaporated as she sank down on the leather sofa. She laid her head back against the cushions as the questions continued to batter her. Should she get dressed and go home? Or should she wait, hoping there was some good reason why Raphael hadn't come? She closed her eyes. Had she lost him? Had he decided she couldn't love if she didn't believe? Her thoughts slowly wound down as the emotional turmoil she'd been living through finally caught up with her. Drifting off to sleep, the final vision in her mind was how Raphael had looked in the moonlight, water dripping from his bronzed body, as he'd walked out of the ocean in Ixtapa. Utterly exhausted, she slept soundly.

Hours later she stretched like a contented cat being stroked. Erotic fantasies filled her dreams: fantasies of Raphael caressing her breasts, of him whispering words of love in her ear, of his hands slipping under the silk of the robe, to touch, to stroke, to arouse her.

Unconsciously Gaby wiggled as the vivid dream sent waves of desire through her. She'd never had a dream like this—hot, sensual, so real she could almost feel the robe slipping from her body, could almost feel the soft sucking of Raphael's mouth as he kissed her breast, could almost feel the thrust of fingers as he found her warm, moist, and ready for

172

his possession. Gaby moaned softly, calling his name as her body arched, seeking fulfillment from the fantasies slowly driving her wild. Her lips parted, her breathing raced, as her dream continued to heat her blood. It seemed so real, she dreamed she could feel the weight of his body pressing her down into the cushions of the sofa. Her pulse pounded as in her fantasy he began to drop butterfly-light kisses on her face, touching every part but her mouth, the one spot that throbbed hungrily with the need for his lips to consume hers.

Gaby moaned softly again; then a sigh of contentment escaped as his mouth finally covered hers, easing the sweet ache. It was the velvety caresses of his tongue, stroking over her lips, plunging to taste the well of sweetness inside, that finally pulled her from the world of fantasy back to reality—a reality that was just as wonderful as the dream.

Slowly her eyes fluttered open and she smiled. "I thought I was dreaming," she whispered, winding her arms about his neck.

"And I was beginning to wonder just what I was going to have to do to wake you up. Your dream might really have gotten sexy if I'd had to wait much longer for my sleeping beauty to awake," Raphael teased, bending down to kiss her again.

There was so much to say, so many questions to be answered, but none of it mattered as she started unbuttoning his shirt. The rest of his clothes rapidly followed his shirt on the floor.

Their union was explosive, as each wanted to burn away the last of the bad memories, leaving only the good. The fire raged so hot, there was no time for a slow arousal, even if either had wanted it. As Raphael's mouth began the fiery plunder of hers; Gaby's hand slid quickly down his chest, not stopping until she found the source of the pleasure that would soon be hers. Without waiting, she guided him into her, desperately needing his plunging conquest to make her happiness complete. He filled her body as love for him filled her heart, and they moved together. She wrapped her legs around him, binding him to her, his arms tightly holding her against the naked length of his body, completing their embrace of love.

Each gave totally, knowing that the passion returned would be just that much sweeter. Bodies glistening with the sweat of their desire, the rhythm speeded until Gaby thought it couldn't get any better; yet, with each thrust into her body, it did. Finally, with a cry pulled from her soul, she accepted the last, the best, the most satisfying, thrust of all as he drove deeply into her, exploding all sensation into a thousand glittering stars. For an exquisite moment they shuddered together and then lay still.

For long moments neither moved; then, with a sigh of complete contentment, she murmured, "Hmmm, that's never happened before. Now I know what they mean by seeing stars."

Raphael propped himself up on one elbow. As she brushed a strand of damp hair from his forehead he said, "Mere stars, my Gabrielle? When you arched against me, driving me deeper and deeper into you, I had skyrockets blasting off in my head."

"Stars, skyrockets, who cares? It was wonderful!" She sighed happily again.

"Does this prove I'm a man, my Gabrielle?"

He asked the question in a light, teasing voice, but she heard the pain underneath. Tears blinded her eyes as she confessed, "Raphael, I would give anything if I could take those words back. I was so terrified of losing you, I just lashed out in fear. I didn't mean it!"

"I know you didn't, my love. I could see that fear in your eyes and knew it was speaking, not you."

She sighed as she admitted, "If anything, it was I who needed to grow up, not you."

His hand cupped her breast. "I've got no complaints. You were plenty 'grown up' a few minutes ago! This is how I want to come home every night, to find my beautiful wife half naked, waiting for me on the sofa."

Gaby's eyes grew round with wonder. "Your wife?" she repeated, hardly daring to believe she'd heard correctly.

"You see, you did it to me again. I'd planned a perfect romantic moment to ask you to marry me, then I looked at you and the words in my heart just slipped out."

A loving hand caressed his cheek. "I think asking me to be your wife after we've just made love is very romantic. Candlelight and champagne couldn't have made it any better. And while we're spreading blame for ruining romantic plans, you ruined my surprise. I wanted you to come home to find me waiting for you, naked in the whirlpool with lust on my mind." She looked at him with a trace of resentment. "But you didn't come home."

"Now, that depends on what home you mean. While you were planning all sorts of debaucheries in my bathroom, I was at your house, waiting with a bottle of champagne and some wicked plans of my own. I saw you across the garage and then suddenly you were gone. I didn't know what had happened. It took a call to Frank to find out you were here." His hand stroked the length of her body. "I'm sure glad we finally found each other, aren't you?"

Gaby moved her hips against him suggestively. "I wouldn't mind 'finding' you again."

"Gabrielle, if you start that, we'll love the night away. We have the rest of our lives for that. Tonight we need to talk." As he eased away from her he wrapped the concealing robe about her. "There, now maybe I'll be able to concentrate. You'll have to admit there's much to say, not to mention the time we need for the surprise I've planned for you."

"Oh, no!" she groaned. "Not another surprise. What is it this time, racing speedboats? Driving in the Indianapolis 500? Jumping out of planes without a parachute?"

"No, it's nothing like that." He chuckled. "This surprise I promise you'll like." His eyes sobered. "No, not just like: I hope you'll love it as much as I do."

"Raphael, I think you've already given me the most important 'surprise.' "

He looked confused. "I don't understand."

"Watching you race was the hardest thing I've ever done in my life. It was hell, but with all my heart I'm glad I did it. It made me face the truth about myself and about us."

"Is that what you meant when you said maybe you were the one who needed to grow up?"

She nodded, trying to find the words to explain what she'd learned about herself. "Sitting there was awful, but the feelings I experienced made me see truths I should have seen long ago." She went on to explain everything she'd felt when she'd watched him cross the finish line.

He was silent as she finished. "It made me realize why I love you with all my soul. It made me realize what you meant when you said we were destined to love. It made me realize that you were right from

176

the beginning: There can be no other man for me. We belong together . . . forever."

"Finally, I know you really are mine." The happiness shining from his eyes was one of the most wondrous things she'd ever seen. Without a word Raphael gathered her into his arms. Their kiss sealed the vow of their love. Before it could develop into anything more, he drew back. "You tempt me, my Gabrielle. When I hold you I can't think. I can only feel, but something else is more important right now."

"Our future?" she whispered. Remembering all his vague reassurances, she silently prayed her doubts would finally be answered as she hesitantly asked, "Can you tell me about it now?"

An almost cocky smile flashed across his face as he vowed, "I can do better than that: I can show you our future." He rolled off the sofa then stood up. "Come on, lazy bones, we've got places to go, and we can't go naked. It goes against every manly instinct I possess, but you'd better get dressed. Otherwise we're never going to get to your surprise."

Still totally in the fog about his plans, Gaby quickly took a shower, then slipped back into her clothes. Raphael was waiting in the living room. "I hate to roust Frank out of bed for the second time tonight to bring the car, but I'm too excited about this to wait."

As he reached for the phone Gaby quickly moved to his side. A slight tremor shook her hand, but that didn't stop her from taking the receiver from him and replacing it. Her eyes met his without wavering. "We don't need Frank."

A lump the size of a golfball sprang into her throat when she saw his dark eyes mist with tears.

"Gabrielle, are you sure? Will you really ride with me again?"

"Maybe that race was the miracle the psychologist talked about. I don't know. I only know one thing: If I could survive watching you race around that track at a hundred-plus miles per hour, I can survive anything! Even riding in your Ferrari."

"It crossed my mind that watching me race and survive might free you of your fears, but I was afraid to hope. With all my heart I'm glad it worked."

"So am I," she agreed with a sigh of relief. "I'll probably still hang on to the armrest for dear life, but I'm ready to go get acquainted with your Ferrari."

Raphael clapped his hands in excitement. "You're going to love her. She can do zero to sixty in—" Suddenly he bit back his words. "Ah, I mean she's a very safe car—special seat belts, a padded dash, an exceptionally safe breaking mechanism, the works!" He spoke quickly to reassure her. When she didn't disagree, his smile returned. "I've got to get something in the bedroom and then we'll be off."

When he returned he had a blanket tucked under his arm. "Don't look at me like that, Gabrielle. This isn't for what you think."

"It isn't? Too bad," she teased. "We're not even married and already you're bored with my love-making."

In three strides he was in front of her. Casting the blanket aside, he swept her into his arms. Like the dashing screen lover, he bent her back until she was helpless to fight off his ravishing kiss even if she wanted to. Neither was breathing evenly when he finally released her.

One fingertip traced over her bruised lips. "You are endlessly fascinating, my love. Not if we are married a hundred years would I tire of holding you, of kissing you, of stripping the clothes from your body. Bore me? Never!"

He glanced at his watch. "But, my temptress, if you don't stop being so seductive, we're going to miss the sunrise. The dawn of a new day, the dawn of our future—I don't want anything to spoil that."

He picked up the blanket, then grabbed the bottle of champagne he'd left on the table. "Now, if you'll get the picnic basket in the kitchen, we'll be ready to go."

"Picnic basket? When did you have time to fix that?"

"When I decided this was how I wanted to celebrate the start of our new life. Now, stop asking questions. We need to go."

Following orders, Gaby found the wicker basket in the kitchen. As she picked it up she wondered what "new life" he was talking about, then shrugged the question away. She had Raphael. She was happy. What else mattered?

Outside she took a deep steadying breath as she looked at the red sports car sitting under the streetlight. If only his Alfa Romeo hadn't also been red! But Gaby didn't hesitate. Raphael's touch gently reassured her as he helped her into the car, then carefully buckled the seat belt in place.

After the first few moments the waves of nausea subsided and her hands began to unclench. Five minutes later she was relaxed enough to notice something peculiar about his driving. She laid a hand on his arm. "Raphael, I'm all right—really I am. I think I could stand going more than twenty miles an hour. At this rate a snail would beat us to your surprise."

He glanced at her out of the corner of his eye. "I didn't want to frighten you."

"I know, and I love you for doing that, but I'm going to be okay," she vowed with a positive shake of her head. "There's just one problem, though: It looks like I'm going to have to give Frank a new job."

Raphael grinned as his foot pushed down gently on the accelerator, bringing the Ferrari up to speed. "I've been talking to Frank, and he's as tired of Big D's traffic as you are. I think I know just the place where he might like to work."

"Where?"

"You'll see."

"Raphael, you really are the most maddening man!" she protested. "All this mystery is driving me nuts."

A wide grin was his only answer as he headed north out of Dallas. The first pink streaks of the approaching dawn were just beginning to lighten the sky when he pulled off the highway onto a dirt road. Nearing the crest of a hill, he stopped. "We're here," he announced, swinging open the car door.

"We're where?" she demanded, automatically following. "This is the middle of nowhere."

He didn't answer as he grabbed the blanket, the picnic basket, and the bottle of champagne, then marched off up the hill.

"The man's crazy!" Gaby muttered, starting after him. After a few yards she had to stop to tap the dirt and small pebbles out of her shoe. When she finally reached the top of the hill, he already had the blanket spread out.

"Oh, Raphael, it's beautiful!" She gasped at her first glimpse of the ranch spread out below. A large herd of cattle grazed peacefully in one field. In another there were a dozen mares with tiny colts romping at their side. But it was the house that took her breath away. Made of white brick, and built around a sunny courtyard filled with flowers, it was so reminiscent of their villa in Saint-Tropez that tears came to her eyes. There was a sign that said SALE PENDING tacked to the fence.

His arm tightened about her waist as he drew her close to him. "When I found it I knew it would be the perfect place to raise our children. Gabrielle, I wanted this for us. That's why I drove in that Grand Prix."

She pulled her gaze away from the beauty below to look at him. A frown furrowed her forehead. "But I don't . . ."

"My love, I have a lot to explain, and I want to give you that explanation as the sun comes up to bless our new home." He took her hand and pulled her down to the blanket. "Come, let me pour you some champagne."

Inside the picnic basket were two crystal glasses, fruit, cheese, and a loaf of the crisp French bread he knew she loved. After pouring the wine, he toasted: "To us, to the future I can finally place at your feet."

Slowly, as they sipped the wine and broke off chunks of bread to savor with the fruit and cheese, she learned the secrets he'd been holding in his heart.

"Gabrielle, I know you wondered why my promises were so vague. They were vague because until I had a chance to drive in the race, I honestly didn't know how I could work things out. I came to Dallas with nothing but my love to offer you and I couldn't give you a future on so little."

"So little? Oh, Raphael, what more would I ever need but your love?"

181

"Love can't give you a home. Love can't take care of you the way you deserve to be cared for. Love can't feed children. But that's all I had."

A rueful smile touched his lips as he confessed. "It's hard for me to admit this, but all the accusations you'd hurled at me three years ago were true. I was wild. I was extravagant. When I finished playing soccer, I'd squandered almost every penny I'd made. Besides losing you, realizing I had nothing to show for my life but a scrapbook of press clippings is what finally made me into a different person from the one you'd known."

She frowned again. "But I still don't understand. The Ferrari, the penthouse, all the money Jean-Claude was paying you—what do you mean love was all you had?"

"Don't you understand? The Ferrari, the penthouse, the wardrobe, the expense accounts, were all part of the deal I made with Jean-Claude. I don't own any of it. If I'd quit representing his line—and believe me, I wanted to do that more than anything in the world—they'd all have disappeared like a puff of smoke. Granted, the job gave me all the glitter; what it didn't give me was enough cash to buy a secure future."

"Raphael, love is sharing. My agency is making a lot of money now. We could have—"

"*No!*" The vehemence in his tone stopped her words cold.

"No," she repeated softly, completely understanding, "you couldn't have accepted that, could you? And I wouldn't have wanted you to."

"Remember what I said: There are some things a man must do to be a man. Never could I have lived on your money, even if you'd had millions. In Spain a man takes care of his family." Suddenly the harsh lines eased from his face as he reached over and ran a loving hand across her stomach. "I hope Margie can manage the agency from time to time, because I want a large family."

She blushed at the thought, then had to admit that the idea of having children, lots of children, by him delighted her. She looked again at the house below, which was just beginning to sparkle in the morning light. She happily visualized the addition of a swing set and maybe a swimming pool off to the left by the oak tree. It was perfect for raising a family. "Is that really going to be ours?" she whispered.

Strong fingers pulled her face back to look at him. "It will be if you'll let me finish this so we can go meet the people and give them the down payment I promised."

"I'm sorry, Raphael. I was just thinking about how wonderful it would be to add a swimming pool and—"

"Isn't that typical. I hand a woman a house of dreams, and immediately she starts redecorating!" He laughed, then his smile faded as his gaze, too, was pulled back to the house below. They were silent a long time, then he continued: "Three years ago you were right. I wasn't ready to settle down. Getting married then would have been a disaster. After you were gone I grew restless. I needed something in my life and it wasn't just your love."

"I'll bet I can guess," she commented, remembering her own return to Dallas. "You needed roots."

"You're as wise as you are beautiful. It took me a long time to realize that. I was raised on a cattle ranch in Spain. My father was a rancher, and my grandfather before him. I guess that tradition fi-

183

nally reached out and drew me back to it. One afternoon, when you were working, I drove out and found this place. Then I knew what I'd been seeking." His voice hardened. "But there wasn't a damned thing I could do about it!"

Hot tears of shame burned her eyes as she stared at him. "I've been so wrong about you. I accused you of loving the spotlight, the glamour of being America's newest sex symbol, when that's not what you wanted at all."

"That, my love, is an understatement. *Dios mío*, how I hated that job! There's only one woman I want 'pawing' me, and that's you. I know I could have gone on with Jean-Claude, but that wasn't the career I wanted. To be happy, I had to find some way out."

"You kept telling me you'd changed. I just didn't have faith to believe you. Can you forgive me?"

He kissed the tears from her cheeks. "There's nothing to forgive. You believed what you saw. I can't blame you for that. There was just so much I couldn't explain. Yet, even when I couldn't see a way to give you the future I wanted for both of us, in my heart I knew somehow I'd get the money to tell Jean-Claude to find another representative for his line."

"And driving in the Grand Prix gave you that opportunity, didn't it?" she asked, the last pieces finally falling into place.

His dark eyes begged her to understand. "I knew that would upset you, but I was trapped. There wasn't anything else I could do. I wanted out of that job, wanted some security for our future, and Ferrari gave me that. They were desperate. Their driver was out with a broken leg, so they came to me. They were already getting a lot of excellent publicity from the car they'd loaned me. Now they saw an even better opportunity to expand their American market. So they offered me a flat two hundred thousand dollars to drive, and a cut of any prize money I won."

"Two hundred thousand dollars," she repeated.

"Don't look so shocked. In the end it was a great deal for them. They got at least that much in free publicity from the deal. Fabian saw to that. So it worked out for everyone."

His hand cupped her face, searching for his own reassurances. "Now do you understand why I had to drive, why I insisted I was driving for you. I was too proud to come to you with nothing. Now I can give you a home. I wanted something secure to build our future on. Not soccer where one missed step can destroy a knee. Not even this deal with Jean-Claude, where I'm this year's sex symbol, if I must use that awful description, who just as easily could be forgotten next year."

"I understand, but I wish you had told me all this before the race."

"I'd planned to, but when you were so frightened, so irrational in your fear, I didn't think it was the time to tell you about all the plans I'd made." His hand swept over the scene below. "You might have been even more afraid if you thought you might lose this too. Besides, I realized there were still a dozen things that might go wrong to ruin everything I'd planned. I wanted to be sure before I brought you here. Do you think you can love a soccer player turned rancher?"

"With all my heart!" She reached up and softly kissed him on the mouth, then drew away. "I just want you to promise me one thing."

"Anything, my Gabrielle."

"Just promise me you will love, honor, cherish . . . and not race!"

A smile, so pure in its love that it stole Gaby's breath away, touched Raphael's lips as he gazed at her. Then, as the sun appeared over the horizon to touch them with its light, he eased her down on the blanket. When she was on her back he bent toward her. As his lips brushed hers in a kiss, his nimble fingers undid the first button of her linen blouse. "I promise to love . . ." he whispered, moving a breath away. ". . . to honor . . ." His kiss returned, claiming hers once more for delightful moments as the second button fell to his quest. ". . . to cherish . . ." he murmured, before returning once more to the delicious tasting of her mouth. As he kissed her his fingers found the third button. ". . . and not to race!" he vowed, propping himself up on one elbow.

Gaby smiled. "I like the way you make promises."

Raphael shook his head doubtfully. "Well, I don't know; a promise isn't any good if it isn't sealed," he commented, reaching behind him.

Gaby giggled as the icy rivulet of champagne trickled down between her breasts, but it never entered her mind to say "Raphael, don't!"

Candlelight Ecstasy Romances™

$1.95 each